D1943359

imprint

Contact: Robert.Balke@web.de

1st English edition: May 2025
Genre: Science Fiction Fantasy
Title also available as e-book on Amazon.

Cover design and inside graphics:
created by Robert Balke with
Images by freepik.
Freepik license with commercial usage rights.
Title-Graphic from shutterstock.com (ID 466398455)

age recommendation 14+

Translation Disclaimer

The story was translated using AI. Therefore, incorrect sentences or content may occasionally occur.

Robert Balke

Gamers

- Stories in Front -

Chapter List

Alien

You could say it was a day like any other. One of those where nothing special or outstanding happened. And on such day, three equally normal boys entered a run-down stairwell.

Evening had already fallen and after the heavy entrance door slammed loudly behind them, they climbed expectantly up one of those typical, multi-story staircases. The walls were emblazoned with hand-painted pictures of gaming heroes. They stood majestically in a victorious pose. Some were as colorful as graffiti, others were dirty and eerie, like something from a darker dream. The weather had made them look old and pale. But that didn't stop the boys from marveling at them every time and wondering loudly which game or story they came from. Now and then one of them pulled out a pen and, as best as the crumbling plaster allowed, added a few sinister figures or improvements to the line. Almost all the heroes and fantasy creatures that had stuck in people's minds were represented in this stairwell. Many were drawn in a wild jumble. Some were even on top of each other, so that from the bottom of the stairs they looked more like a colorful mush of breakfast cereal. Some were from some manga comics. Bright pink lettering and garish neon combined with the colors of the superheroes. A little further up, there were the dark and evil figures, who also had a place here. Some of them looked scary, but the scariest of them was at the top of the entrance door. A creature with a huge mouth and sharp fangs rushed towards you. Slimy and wide open, a pitch-black maw formed, with the entrance to an Alien located right in the middle.

The *Alien* was nothing more than a computer club. There were many such clubs in the city, and they were a magnet for bored kids thirsting for action and company. Here you could meet, exchange ideas, and pursue common interests. This is what

prompted the three boys to stop by every time. One of them would bang on the entrance door and then you had to wait until someone moved behind it. But you couldn't expect nice interiors or anything like that here. That was because behind this door you focused on the essentials and that was gaming. And without sugarcoating things, in this club you also met the losers. Because among the kids who were there during the day to avoid school there were also the guys without a steady job, without goals or plans and with problems of all kinds. People who couldn't handle the pressure, as they called it, and hadn't really found their place in society. Or there was simply no suitable place for them.
On the streets, some who visited the Alien were insulted as bums or addicts. But in the club, it was different. Here such people also found recognition. In this place, their addictive behavior was even celebrated, and the word *"addict"* was therefore also used as a compliment, not like a swear word. Something that was happily given with a genuine laugh. That was the *Alien*.
Where the failures, losers, bums, and addicts were concentrated in one place. And the trend was increasing. Nevertheless, it was completely fine for the boys.
Suddenly the door moved. A heavy bolt went back. But it only opened a crack. A man with a puffy face and beads of sweat on his forehead peeked out and asked grumpily for money. One of the three then pulled a crumpled bill out of his pocket and with a loud squeak, the dark maw opened to the Alien.

Inside, a stuffy, unbearable heat spread. Days before, the sudden arrival of summer had already caused the city's residents a lot of trouble, and the gamers who were now playing here around the clock were actually making the heat wave even worse. This club was too poor and run-down for anyone to even dare to talk about air conditioning. Therefore, they had no choice to stick the small windows shut with scraps of paper to completely block out the annoying sunlight. In addition, several fans had to be used, which were attached in the most unlikely places so that they

didn't completely dissolve in their own juice. It goes without saying that not only the heat, but also the stench that had now boiled up, defied all description. But the guys were, as they themselves always emphasized, "basically pain-free" in this respect and headed for their usual seats without hesitation.
All you had to do was log in, using a password and wait for the title screen of your chosen game. The controls needed for this were completely embedded in the table, as with any modern computer, so that there was enough space for books and other writing materials. The actual computer was therefore no longer visible. All the power was no longer handled on-site but managed by external servers that processed all the incoming input and output signals at breakneck speed. So even here in this run-down club, there was just a bunch of glowing screens and users clicking wildly. That was all.

The three boys were called Jury, Max and Finn and were euphorically playing a new computer game. It was called *Infinity* and the latest thing on the gaming market. One of the usual upcoming trends. So, nearly everyone was playing it.
The greetings from the others, who also spent their evenings here in this musty *alien* room, were rather poor. Because every little distraction could mean the death of the gamer. Thus, they quickly exchanged a few casual phrases, such as:
"Hey, here again," "What's up?", or "Back to get yourselves cooked?" Then came sayings like: "Fu*k you," or "Sure, you bum." A laugh here and there, a cool gesture, a sip from a colorful drink can, a quick high-five with the regular gamers, and then everyone sat down in their usual place without much ado and started.
It was like that every evening now. As soon as dusk fell on the small, winding streets, it became, as one of the boys summed it up in one word, uncomfortable. Only when the night was over, and the early morning appeared with a low sun in the reddish sky was it safe to head home. By this time, all the amateur criminals,

drunks and junkies had long since fallen into a deep sleep of booze-drugs and were no longer a threat to the normal people. Some hated the city because of this. Others loved it and raved about it wherever they could. About its lifestyle, the architectural style of the center, the attitude of the people and so on. But Jury, Max and Finn didn't worry about it. They didn't know any different and one could now tell where they came from and what brought them to these crowded streets. But to make a long story short: The three were so-called street kids. Their parents were simply absent for various reasons and left the upbringing of their offspring to the loud city people.

L..O..S..E..R

Jury had long, blond hair and was still wearing the overly baggy trousers he was picked up in somewhere in the center of town. The same was true of Max, except for his jet-black hair and the cap of a not-so-successful football club. Their first encounter was a coincidence.

At a busy intersection, Max had missed a red light and immediately got into an argument with a policeman. Jury happened to observe the scene and was amazed at how the boy managed to get out of trouble with the police officer. He rapped a happy little song to him that went something like this:
"*No, noo, I'm not bad kind, I'm just fu*king colorblind,* " he sang, while the policeman, surprised by this performance, tried to write down his name. But when he then heard another serenade on the topic of "*Red and green, what colors are those?",* he actually let go of him and got back into his vehicle, annoyed. This made such an impression on Jury that he immediately stuck to Max's heels. At first, Max wasn't so enthusiastic about it, but when they came up with more verses out of boredom like:
"*Is it still green or is it already red? Whatever, I'd rather step on the gas until someone is dead.* He and Jury became friends straight away and when Finn joined them in a park some later, there were three of them from then on. They shared their crazy sense of humor and the fact that they had to cope in the hustle and bustle of the city without parents.

Jury was the youngest of the three and despite his age, he was rather small and scrawny compared to some of the others. Finn and Max, on the other hand, were a bit taller and more powerfully built and their recently started puberty was already showing its typical features. So, Jury had to assert himself every time the two of them managed to find something to eat so that he didn't lose all his weight and stay that small forever.

Things were different in the *Alien*. There, Jury was a celebrated gamer. His quick reactions, nimble little fingers and ambition were notorious. After all, nobody wanted to be outdone by a younger guy, no matter how banal the game was. Everyone wanted him on their team and since Infinity came along, Jury was unstoppable when it came to shooting fools and monsters. Infinity quickly became his favorite ego shooter, which increasingly annoyed Max and Finn, who had less success there. This continued until Finn teamed up with someone from the net and won more and more often.

"This guy is great," he said from his station. The others only looked up briefly and continued clicking wildly on their boards.

"Don't be annoying," Jury shot back, never once taking his eyes off screen, and reloading his weapon. But it didn't help. With each new battle, Finn gained more points and his self-confidence seemed to grow, making him even more difficult to defeat.

“Fu*k,” was all you could hear from Max. “Fu*k fu*k, damn it!” The cursing went on until the other gamers also got up from the table out of curiosity.

"What's going on?" someone asked, coming over. Annoyed, Jury explained that Finn had secretly formed an alliance and that the latter was moving unusually fast. That was literally all, but that was enough to finally tear Jury's nerves apart. The gamer, who like the boys wasted his time exclusively with Infinity, looked over Jury's shoulder for a moment until he suddenly started laughing: "No wonder he's getting the better of you," he said, "He's a Realgamer from the Forrester clan." Some people in the room now stood up and watched the fight the three of them were putting up. Jury and Max clicked so quickly that the keys started to click loudly, without even once losing sight of the enemy.

“Man, of course it’s one of the Forresters,” one agreed, while Jury just shrugged helplessly and carried on playing, sweating.

“You have no chance against him,” someone else interjected.

“Why is that?” whispered Jury, whose face had now completely taken on the color of his screen.
“You idiot,” said another spectator. “That’s a Realgamer. You don’t play with them.” And with that sentence the fight ended and a big malicious

L..O..S..E..R

flashed across Max and Jury's screen.

Real- and Stationgamers

It had a conciliatory effect when Finn admitted that same evening that he had teamed up with a Realgamer. After all, there was no shame in losing to someone like that. His friends knew that too, but Stationgamers, which included the three of them and everyone else in the Alien, always stayed among themselves. It didn't really make sense to play together, as the gaming style of these two types of gaming was fundamentally different. Stationgamers were those who played on the PC or a similar stationary device in the usual way. Realgamers, on the other hand, were the others. Those who spent their time exclusively in Augmented Reality, so easily called AR. This inevitably led to the resulting communities facing each other with a certain hostility, with each considering themselves to be the better side. So, the lost fight against a Realgamer caused new emotions and loud talk to boil over in the Alien.
"I'm telling you", someone said, sounding hurt, and sharing his thoughts. "The game between them and us is not balanced at all. Often there is such a delay that it knocks you off in the most impossible ways. Even an unfavorable respawn is enough to make you sticky. Just a crappy income behind your top lane and the whole thing snowballs. And you know me, you know my skill," he said. "I was obviously completely enraged at first. Then I pushed into the middle of his base and back again. He was already weak at that point, but because of the short time to kill rate, he carried all the buffs into his game. All the perks I had earned up to that point couldn't dodge anything. That's how it is with these guys. Total upfu*k, I tell you."
“You said it,” another agreed, and the conversation continued. Meanwhile, Finn silently looked at his chat window. The Realgamer had written him a message there:

Hey, not bad at all...for a SG xD
":P Sure", Finn wrote back.
We could really use someone like you.
Finn paused and needed a moment to come up with an appropriate answer:
"Well, RG isn't really my thing. I haven`t money for that and I'm already out with my friends."
With your skill level you shouldn't bother with SGs. ;D And as for the money, there's always a way that can be done.
"...don't know", typed Finn.
Your friends can join in too. If you want to be there, we really should meet up. What do you say?

Finn stared thoughtfully through the screen. So, it took a while until he quietly called Max and Jury over and mysteriously showed them what the Realgamer had written. Finn suddenly felt no longer averse to the offer and suggested that they at least try it out. But Max and Jury felt taken by surprise. They couldn't get used to playing under different leadership, in a completely different team. Especially not when they were Realgamers. Because they were usually snobby rich kids that no street kid wanted to compete with, but there were also strange, even bizarre stories about realgaming. Insiders said it was dangerous and unpredictable and some others were even said to have died. But no one could really say whether all this was true or fake. Jury in particular remained skeptical. The differences were simply too great. Stationgamers, also sometimes abbreviated as *SGs*, keep to themselves. A well-known motto that was pinned in big letters on the Alien's wall and repeated loudly by Jury among the others. But shortly afterwards Max also started talking to him. He illustrated the clan's successes using a high-resolution graphic from the net.
It turned out that the *Forrester's*, as their clan was known in the gaming community, had already bagged amazing trophies, and had achieved incredibly high levels of experience points, coins,

raids, rankings, and special marks in Infinity. These stats even left Jury speechless. Google also spat out countless blogs mentioning them. Followed by streams, blogs and even strategies that were simply referred to as *Forrester moves.* Their level of fame was considerable.

It is not clear to say exactly what caused Jury to give in. Perhaps the Forrester's online presence had left a lasting impression on him? Perhaps it was the fear of losing his best friends in a trivial argument about real and stationary gamers? Or was it really time, as Finn whined, to risk something new instead of hanging out in the filthy Alien every day? All possible thoughts that finally made him give in.
"We can give it a try," he whispered, still skeptical, and so they wrote back together and agreed to meet the following Wednesday. They wanted to meet at the entrance to Central Station to discuss one thing or another in more detail. Shortly afterwards, the word *"daring"* appeared in the chat, so Finn asked with big question marks. The Realgamer explained that they would of course have to prove themselves first to be accepted into the clan. Finn immediately wanted to know more details about this test of courage, but the Realgamer dismissed it. He didn't have the time right now and would explain everything else later, and with that, contact broke off again. Each of them exchanged questioning glances.
“So, it’s a dare.” Finn hissed thoughtfully, and Max shrugged his shoulders helplessly.
“Hmm... then Wednesday”, he replied.
"Yes, Weds", Finn repeated and looked expectantly at Jury, who was silent for a moment. Until he too sheepishly agreed:
“Yes...Wednesday then.”

City of Strayers

The skyscrapers stretched far above the houses of the city. They stood out from a strange yellowish haze and were built so high and spacious that you would think they were only a few minutes' walk away. But if you actually wanted to reach one of these monsters, you would have to set aside a few hours.
Jury, Max and Finn were on their way home. It was already early morning and as always, after the Alien had finally closed its doors, they walked through the streets of their district. Now at this hour, it seemed to belong to them. They crossed closed shops, public squares with park benches littered with rubbish, empty streets, and narrow and winding alleys where people were spreading horrible smells, cursing, spitting and babbling gibberish. But now at this time of day, everything was quiet. No cars or bicycles to be seen or their annoying honking and ringing to be heard. Only the pigeons were cooing wildly and fighting over a whirling piece of bread paper with a colorful advertising slogan.

In the part of town where the boys lived, there were completely dilapidated and destroyed houses. From the street, you could see directly into some of the apartments where people actually lived. And if you stared at them, they would silently and angrily pull a blanket over the broken windows so that you couldn't see inside anymore.
Behind the wide streets, which kept making sudden turns, you had to go through a park. This was where the punks hung out at night. With their crazy clothes and hairstyles, they often argued with other park occupiers.
They then shouted insults at people, smelling of alcoholics, and threatened them with beatings or the bites of a large fighting dog.

There were far too many dogs in the city anyway. One night, one of them was rummaging around in the garbage in front of Jury's sleeping place and grabbed a half-eaten chicken. Jury was scared at first, but the dog soon made off quietly and secretly. And the boys did exactly the same as this stray dog. Because when the three of them found something edible somewhere, they didn't think twice, they grabbed it and made off as quickly as they could.

At the end of another row of houses that ran through the neighborhood like a vein, a street musician was sleeping on a landing. His head was resting on an old violin and the gentle morning wind swept his snoring through the streets, which were also deserted here. His hair and beard were already shaggy and gray. His leather jacket was worn out and much too big for his gaunt shoulders. As the boys approached, he suddenly stirred. But he only melancholy turned his body from one side to the other, where he continued to sleep soundly. Finn indicated with a wave of his hand that this guy was harmless and stepped past. The others did the same and so they continued walking through a long-forgotten housing estate and reached their hiding place.

This accommodation consisted only of the dilapidated upper floor of an empty stairwell. But it was perfectly adequate for the three friends who were resting there after long nights of gaming in the Alien. Even before they took possession, they always spent the nights somewhere else. Constantly looking for food and a safe place. A place where they wouldn't be chased away at night or possibly even picked up by the police.
But ever since Finn discovered this abandoned upper floor, things had gotten better for them. Nobody was bothered by the fact that three boys lived at the end of the stairs, where the only way was to the roof trusses that were no longer weatherproof. Boys who occasionally played cards on the broken floorboards under a lamp hanging from a cable or drove off their hunger and

tiredness. They just had to be quiet enough. Because a few floors below, a hunchbacked woman still lived. They estimated her age, like the rings of trees, by the number of wrinkles on her face. One hundred and twenty was the unanimous answer. She bred a flock of cats in the basement of the house. That was also where people went to the toilet now and then. But cats were still better than rats in the house. Everyone agreed on that. But the boys never really stayed long. They usually just spent their mornings there. Maybe longer if it was stormy outside or the rain wouldn't stop. With the help of some stolen mattresses, they had built a kind of oversized nest at the bottom of the stairs and now, after a meal of pasta with leftover sauce, they lay down, tired and exhausted. They shared a few leftovers, exchanged a few thoughts, buried themselves deep in the soft blankets and fell asleep. There were many like the three of them in the city. The boys were strayers.

Begging and its rules

The sun burned the asphalt of the streets. Stone, concrete, and metal heated each other up in the never-ending play of light from midday sun. The boys were thirsty and hungry. So, they were now in the largest shopping area in their district, begging for a quick meal among the harried residents of the city. Finn had grabbed a coffee mug and was strolling through the crowds. In waves, people moved through the narrow shopping arcades of small shops, stores, snack stands, cafes and bars. Past colorful advertising banners and cardboard cutouts. Then fruit sellers who loudly and intrusively advertised the freshness of their goods. Followed by musicians, showmen, acrobats, and self-proclaimed artists. And even dubious street vendors who traded in front of the oversized department stores and their fully automatic glass entrances. It was unbelievable what kind of people you met in these hidden corners. In between the boys. Just as active, just as busy.

While Jury asked the people walking by to donate, Max tried his hand at the so-called *heel-ripper* for the first time. Finn had thought it up and promised a sure-fire deal. Although Finn was very successful at begging, he felt that a new trick was always needed. This was the only way to lure money out of people's pockets with a certain degree of consistency, he said, and explained his new trick like this:

First, you would look for a particular stretch of road. Preferably one where distinguished lady in high heels were constantly crossing your path. Then you just needed an old ventilation grate and placed it so that the ladies' heel would get caught in it. If this was the case, you just had to step in and help them if they accidentally lost their way or got stuck. You could usually expect a generous donation. And if the women were even accompanied by a noble gentleman, you could be sure that a little help would bring in a decent amount of cash. You just had to hold out your

hand to the man and wait for a fair payment. He wouldn't dare refuse a donation. Otherwise, the nice company would be over. "It works best with people who are newly in love," said Finn, who perfected the begging among the three of them. According to him, this also had its own rules that had to be followed. For example, there was something like:
Never be unfriendly. Be conspicuous and speak directly. Make them feel like they have done something good. Shower people with praise. A small trick will attract attention. Choose your location carefully. It is best to do it where people still have their wallets to hand and where no one else is already begging. Because people rarely want to donate a second time. And once you have earned a lot of money, get out of there quickly. After all, there are always enough envious people on the streets.
Such rules were nothing new to Max, but he still had some doubts about the heel-ripper and expressed the problem: How could one tell whether someone was newly in love or whether the couple was in an intact relationship?
"Don't talk bullshit," said Finn and told Max to finally try it out.

Max placed the grate, which he had stolen from a floor ventilation system, in a suitable place and waited. But after a while he had to realize that none of the women were, well, let's say, "stupid" enough to fall into his trap. Because each of them, always steered past it at the very last moment, or stepped over it with a surprisingly large step. Max quickly lost patience with such things, that at some point he headed towards a heavily laden woman to gently maneuver her towards the bars. Okay, maybe it was a little shove. Who could say it between all those people? In any case, the woman stumbled across the bars and her full bags flew through the air in a wide arc. The woman shouted at Max, asking what the whole thing was about, and at the same moment she lost her balance because of her high heels. She rushed straight towards Max and, after a not very graceful stumbling step, simply buried him under her. Finn, who had been watching

closely from a distance, pulled Jury towards him and both immediately ran over. They looked at the situation in disbelief. Because Max was nowhere to be seen under the woman. Only when she tried to get up did a muffled cry for help come from below her. To save Max from suffocating to death, Jury and Finn had to lend her a hand. But the expected donation did not come. On the contrary, because as soon as she regained even a little of her balance, she immediately started cursing. Finn countered that the woman was responsible for his friend's death and threatened, between Max's pain-distorted groans, with a hefty insurance claim. Jury did not fully understand what that meant, but he knew one thing for sure: all Finn did not have was insurance that covered such situations in any way. The woman made an angry face that grew more and more swollen, and Finn did not let up in order to somehow assert his right to "appropriate compensation". It was fascinating how he threw the rules he had just praised overboard himself. Never being unfriendly was supposedly the most important thing and Jury was amazed at how unfriendly Finn's arguments could become. But the woman did not let that intimidate her. She fired back just as venomously, making people stop and form a crowd of curious looks.
“Hey, I know that guy,” someone suddenly shouted from the crowd. “He often rips people off here. You must be careful.”
At that moment, Finn made a face that Max and Jury knew exactly how to interpret. It was time to get out of here. And so, it only took a moment for the three to take off. Each of them dashed in a different direction and tried to dig deep into the crowd. That was the surest way to create the necessary confusion, avoid being pursued and caught. Jury ran as fast as he could and repeatedly bumped into unsuspecting passers-by.

There were two men with thick glasses staring around, sullen and confused. Right behind them, ladies in elegant dresses, with striking make-up and a trailing cloud of perfume. Closely followed

by a flock of poodles barking on a pink dog leash. Jury had to jump to avoid falling and with each new attempt, the people rushed past faster.
Businessmen in suits and ties. Then construction workers with fresh rolls. A woman in a whirring wheelchair. A postman with packages. A short man with a hip-hop cap. Four loud-mouthed young people. Three girls with shopping bags. A woman with a child, wearing a fur coat despite the heat. A boy with a gold chain around his neck. Three painters with sunburn. A toddler with a lollipop. A girl with a scooter. An overweight couple eating ice cream. A guy with his hair teased up, snow-white sneakers and an Indian chief on his shirt. A shop owner stressed out at work. A woman on the phone, discussing the previous weekend. Then another. Followed by two portly men, laughing loudly about something. Another lady with a dog and familiar sunglasses. (Seems to be fashionable now.) A rickety motorcycle shoots past. A pickup truck tries to park. Someone honks. A window in the sea of houses opens. One calls, another answers. All of this flashed past Jury like slow motion as he continued running without looking back.

Luckily, the three friends had identified an emergency meeting point for exactly such unexpected cases. Not far from a kiosk that only sells sports magazines and dirty booklets sold, there was a pedestrian bridge that led over loudly screeching freight traffic. That was exactly where everyone met up again. You could see the whole city from here and it was also a cool place to just hang out. The only person who didn't like this place was Finn. That was because he was afraid of heights. So, he never sat right at the edge and didn't want to admit it.
Jury, Max, and Finn laughed loudly. They had calmed down at the meeting point and the people here had not noticed all the recent commotion. Max was sitting on one of the many concrete pillars and leafing through a glossy football magazine. He caught up on the latest information about his club and surprisingly threw the

two of them a couple of cereal bars. They were surprised where the money suddenly came from. Max confessed that he had reached into the woman's pockets while she was lying on top of him and had actually pulled out a tenner. He grinned, imitated a delicate feeling movement, and made it clear that this was his way of getting money. But Finn only felt confirmed that the tricks he thought up always worked sooner or later. But Max had had enough of his ideas and insisted on sticking with the traditional methods for today. Because they worked quite well, he said. And so, it wasn't long before the three of them went about their usual daily business again, waiting for one coin after another to fall into their cup.

Although this method worked particularly well for Finn, he often talked about better and faster ways to make money. Of course, kids always had an advantage over the large number of beggars who roamed the city, but sooner or later even the best tricks and gimmicks were known and perceived by passers-by as dirty tricks. And it was simply bad for business if someone shouted, "You little crooks!" or something similar. That's why he always had to come up with something new, he explained. But despite all the tricks, his undisputed success was not only down to his cleverness. His innocent smile, his lovely facial features, coupled with large, chestnut-brown eyes and his exuberant charm also influenced the people passing by. Finn's trademark was also his plain hoodie, the baggy hood of which he rarely took off between people. Only now did the sun reveal his mocha-colored skin and wildly disheveled hair. Add to that his snub nose and his sparkling white teeth, which made his smile stand out even more.

Crabs

Midday was already over when the three made their way to the edge of town. Despite the small incident with the failed heel-ripper, they had at least managed to quench their hunger and thirst. Jury pulled the collar of his shirt over his nose to distance himself for a moment from the thousand smells that the city was spreading. While Max and Finn counted the money they had begged for again, they continued on with determination. There was still something important to do. Because before they could take their dare with the Realgamers, before they could go on the expedition, they still had to make some preparations. They still didn't know what to expect and their speculations escalated almost hourly, but Finn's contact had sent some rough instructions that at least gave them an idea of what they had to prepare for the following day.

In a spacious square with ancient statues and dried-up fountains, they explained once again the reason for their detour to the outskirts of the city.
"We should really stop by there. They always have something," said Max and Finn, while Jury followed them along a crowded promenade. Further and further, deeper and deeper into an unmanageable swamp of people and their constant goings-on. Hours must have passed when they finally reached the long, high concrete wall. It cut through the wide area of the city belt and the high wall of rough and misshapen stones was already casting long shadows over the adjacent buildings. Jury only knew this place from stories. Walls that were too high, strange tales, and an underlying fear, had kept him away from here until then. But his friends headed for the mighty entrance gate without hesitation to enter for a small fee.
An unkempt man in a linen robe with holes in it and a sun hat guarded the entrance. His teeth were frighteningly black and

crooked. His breath crept into your nose like a foul wind and Max blurted out the words that others were only thinking:
"Crab," Finn then gave him a warning nudge in the side and as her counted money jingled into the guard's bowl, he puffed on a tobacco pipe and smiled contentedly. The gate, which reminded Jury of two mighty wings, finally opened with a loud creak via a large lever mechanism.

It was a garbage dump where the *Crabs* lived. Crabs was what they called the garbage diggers. People who made a simple living from the garbage of others, the better-off people. Not a nice thought, but that was the way things were when hunger and poverty dominated a large part of the city. You couldn't sink any lower than a Crab here. It was the lowest level of life a person could imagine. That's why the name *Crab*, which was often used as a swear word in the city, was very unpopular behind these walls, Finn said. It was better to swallow it.
The man, whose appearance was reminiscent of a well-travelled vagabond, had assigned the boys an area with the words “4B”. That was exactly where they were allowed to search. Several signs marked the narrow paths and trails, on the edges of which mountains of garbage were piled up. Urban garbage was the word that the jury in amazement as he trotted after Max and Finn.

The Crabs processed everything that the city no longer needed. Whether it was a refrigerator, a TV or a sofa, everything that prosperity spat out ended up here.
Packaging as far as the eye could see. In between, small black clouds of smoke that gave off a pungent stench. Through the dubious haze, there was no end to the sugarloaf-like towers of plastic tubs, household items and electronic waste. Old cars, streetlamps, park benches, traffic lights. The Crabs had obviously already sorted them. While Jury marveled at this strange place with wide eyes, Finn was looking purposefully for a "4B". Max, on

the other hand, kept stopping at fantastically bizarre structures and stumbling through the things that had strayed down from above back onto the small paths. Jury was also infected by his hunting fever and every time someone thought they had found something interesting, Finn stopped, pressed his hand on their chest, shook his head with a serious expression and pointed to an idle man not far away. Away from the towers, this seemed to be keeping watch and until they reached location 4B, it was impossible to rummage around here without danger. Because what at first glance appeared to be insignificant rubbish still seemed to have considerable value for the people here. Max and Jury now understood this too and so they continued.

There was an incredible amount of electronics on display at this location. Yes, whole mountains of cables, circuit boards and bent metal sheets. The jury asked if anyone knew what it was.
"These are all computer parts," said Finn, explaining that they were once among the thousands of PCs that the people of the city used every day. Jury could not imagine that there was a time when everyone had their own static computer. What a waste. Demands had grown so much that it no longer made much sense to put them all into one device. The focus was now more on using the cloud, which was much more economical for everyone and could be designed to meet their needs.
This meant that you could easily choose your CPU performance or memory capacity or adjust it according to your needs.

It took a while until they found their assigned spot. Unfortunately, for the few cents they had thrown into the vagabond's bowl, location 4B was appropriate. A relatively tiny pile of various small and scrap parts, which probably came from the buildings in the center that were being demolished, lay before them for their search. All three were hoping for handy heating pipes or at least something similar, which they could only find there in such a short time. For their dare, they needed some kind of holder. Realgamers used this for their trigger chip. It went without saying that this holder should resemble a firearm in shape and form. The trigger chip, which recorded the position and number of shots fired, was then attached to the appropriate spot using a screw, nail, or glue. Only then could the game be played in a *shooter-like* manner. There were no limits to the improvised weapons. Whether welded pipes, old bicycle handlebars, glued plastic or even wooden slats, everything was possible. Nevertheless, the guys agreed that their look should at least be something special and so they spent another hour pulling something suitable out of the pile of junk.

Max had a lot of fun doing this. Every time he thought he had discovered something great, he immediately pulled and tugged at it. This caused Finn and Jury, who were climbing a little higher up, to stumble dangerously.
"Watch out man", they shouted, and held on tight at the right moment as a surprisingly large part came loose and crashed loudly to the ground. Horrified, Jury looked over the countless spikes, sharp-edged metal pieces and knife-like bars that had narrowly missed him. Clearly, the life of a crab was dangerous. Help was unlikely to arrive quickly in this unreal place. So, from then on everyone remained cautious and concentrated on the things that were easier to reach.
Now and then a few crabs looked over from distance. Only their silhouettes could be seen because the sun was already low in the sky. Only when a cloud moved in front of the red sun did it become clear that it was actually a woman with a child. Barefoot and wearing nothing but a few torn rags, they looked over at us inquisitively. Jury became thoughtful.
Life here was marked by an unimaginable poverty. Old men, women, and children. Dressed in dirty clothes, they rummaged through the stinking garbage of the people who lived beyond these high walls. Toxic, dirt, and chaos were words that aptly described the surroundings. So Jury was especially happy when

his friends unanimously suggested that they leave this place as soon as dusk fell. And when they left the mighty entrance gate behind them some later and the familiar surroundings of the city spread out before them, Jury was able to breathe a sigh of relief for the first time.

Happy and satisfied, everyone admired their souvenirs once again. Jury had got hold of two pipes screwed together, which he combined with a matching rod handle. Max secured a bolt gun that no longer works, which used to be used to fire long nails into wooden boxes. And although Finn's search took the longest, his haul was rather meager. But it was enough for a sparkling aluminum structure with a questionable spring mechanism, which he presented with satisfaction.
They still had a long way to go back, so Finn didn't have to do much convincing to get the others on one of the trams. Usually, you needed a ticket for this, but the boys knew a secret place where the lock that controlled access to the platform was faulty. All you needed was an old day ticket and a felt-tip pen. If you knew the code printed on it, which you cracked via Internet, you just scribbled over certain parts and voilà: you were granted free travel on the tram.

Inside, the picture of busy people repeated itself. Whether standing or sitting, almost everyone was busy with themselves until they reached the desired destination. Many had just come from work. You could see it in their faces, which stared into space, sluggish and exhausted. Others were listening to loud music while chewing gum, talking on the phone, or chatting. And others were so engrossed in a book that they showed no emotion. Not even when the train took a sharp bend, as it did now, in order to drive up a small bridge with more momentum. Just for a moment, you could see into the illuminated windows. Where a woman with a raised index finger was just reprimanding

a little girl, or where a frail man was statue-like taking a cup out of the kitchen cupboard.
At the end of the bridge, which once again extended deep into the traffic, Jury was in a state of shock. At the next stop, a uniformed man had got on and it took Jury a moment to realize that fortunately it was not a policeman. It was just a fat security guard. Like many others, he was probably already off work. Nevertheless, he tried to avoid his gaze and when the man got off again after another stop and Jury felt safe again, he flinched again. Because a woman was sitting not far away. It was the woman they had bullied so much that morning in the shopping area. And before she spotted one of the boys, Jury warned the others with a quick finger gesture. To avoid their gaze, Finn pulled the hood of his hoodie further down over his face and Jury slid just as far down in the seat so as not to be in their field of vision. Max was the only one who didn't mind. He just stared back provocatively. But there was no conflict. At the next stop she left the train and more passers-by pushed through the door.

With each new station, peace returned. Between the rows of seats, Jury noticed a group of students. At the end of the carriage, they were laughing and talking. They had to be students because the characteristics were clear. Their conversation was about lessons, teachers, recess, and exams. Here and there, a book changed hands. Jury eyed their appearance shyly. From their shoes to their hair, everything was well-groomed. Not a single stain or tear on their clothes. It had been a while since any of the boys had attended school. Behind each of them, why and how this was so, was a personal story. You could now tell how it all happened, but not everyone was immediately ready to lay out their problems and troubles in front of the others. It was also good to just push such things aside and forget them, at least for a while. And when someone asked uncomfortable questions about education, they avoided them as best they could or replied defiantly, like Max:

"School? That's not for us."

After most of them had left the tram, Max and Finn noticed Jury's gaze, which was still fixed on the students at the end of the tram. They didn't let on, but both, like him, fell into a thoughtful mood. They couldn't pinpoint the exact reason, but with the streetlights now gradually coming on, tomorrow and with it the dare was getting closer and closer. For the rest of the journey, the three of them stared out the window in silence, where the lights of the city were reflected.

Ox

People were milling around in front of the station. There were several such travel stations in the city, but this one was the biggest and called itself Central Station because it was simply in the center of the city.
Everywhere you looked there were harried travelers with heavy bags and the typical where-to-now faces. Unfamiliar faces mixed in with farewell scenes from all sorts of people. Normally a perfect place for the boys to hang out and dust themselves off. They had often enough passed the time here. They practiced begging people or parcel-belt surfing. That's what they called the illegal use of parcel-belts that transported heavy luggage from A to B along the edge of a staircase. The ones that ran deep down were particularly fun. You then had to keep your balance, like surfing, so as not to fall between all the suitcases. People always made horrified faces or cursed loudly. But today there was no time for that. Jury, Max, and Finn were lost in the crowd this time. Like many others, they waited in the mighty entrance hall, for the big clock to finally show the full hour. Their meeting point was aptly chosen. A special place had to be found that spoke for itself in terms of size and conspicuousness. The three of them were waiting in front of a meter-high Infinity poster, which had been found everywhere since the release. The city was literally plastered with this type of advertising. Often, on the streets or on desolate remains of walls, you could also find simple sayings like "Become a legend" in exaggeratedly bold letters. Even house-sized graffiti in meter-high letters, which spelled out the word Infinity, could be found here and there between busy blocks of houses.
Without a doubt, this left a lasting impression on all the kids who spent their free time there every day.

The boys were puzzling over what exactly was shown on the poster in the entrance hall. Finn said that this was from the last level and explained it with the help of background, which showed a magnificent starry sky with galaxies. Max and Jury saw it differently and eagerly discussed the gamers fighting there. In their opinion, the armor and weapons depicted were far too low-quality and could not possibly be used in the very last stage. Finn countered with purely loud arguments, but before they could come to a reasonable agreement, they were spoken to from behind. Someone approached them with a hesitant "Hey". And this someone was a strangely conspicuous person whose name in this story only had two letters. He called himself *Ox*.
"Are you the Stationgamers?", was heard among the people, so that our three turned around at the same time. In front of them stood a slender but tall boy. Like Max, he had black hair, but he wore it in a distinctive spiky hairstyle. It had recently become fashionable and anyone who stood out from the crowd simply had to wear it.
The spiky hairstyle involved twisting individual strands of hair together and letting them stick out wildly in all directions. And then it was finished. But it wasn't just his hair that was unusual, everything else was too.
Although the light in the reception hall was normal, the boy was wearing shimmering blue mirror sunglasses. Like in a spy film, he looked through them first to the left and right, then mysteriously over them and examined the boys. Only now did it become apparent that he was wearing dark make-up around his eyes, but this did not disguise his clearly Asian facial features. His clothing, however, was a little less conspicuous, but strangely combined. For example, he wore biker gloves. The kind that only reached to the knuckles. Then a dark green army vest, with worn shoulder pieces and frayed sleeves. Underneath a shirt with the inscription: *FUC* Y All*
A little further down, a pair of equally worn but normal trousers peeked out. Over them, however, he was wearing shin guards,

like those you would see in football. He also had on the corresponding shoes with the clacking studs and looked as if he had sprinted here straight from training. But when Max immediately commented: "Cool, you play football?", he just shook his head in surprise and fiddled with the backpack he had brought with him. Only after all three had looked this strange boy up and down did they answer his question:
“Yes, the Stationgamers, that’s us. Are you Ox?” said Finn.
"Of course, I am", the boy replied flippantly, and without any of the usual greeting banter, he got straight to the point. He took off his backpack and rummaged through its contents.

Ox, even his name was strange. Of course, in the gaming world you could adopt any name you liked, but using the nickname in everyday life was rather strange even for the boys, so Max insisted and asked again with raised eyebrows:
“And your name is really Ox?” he asked, “just Ox?”
"Sure, damn it," he replied with extreme venom, looking nervously in all directions as if the people walking past, with all their unpredictable movements, were overwhelming him. While he was still rummaging around in his backpack, he asked:
“Tell me, what school do you actually go to?”
"Well, we don't go to school anymore," Finn replied. The boy paused for a moment and now looked suspiciously over his glasses.
“But you’re not outcast freaks or anything?” he said.
“No no,” the three laughed.
“It’s a long, weird story,” Max interjected, causing Ox to give everyone another critical look.
"Hmm..." he said, and with a somewhat perplexed shrug of his shoulders, he finally said, "Okay," and didn't go into it any further, but pulled a worn-out bag out of his backpack. Inside was something that amazed the three of them. Out came two pairs of Google glasses, which the boys accepted speechlessly. None of them had held one in their hands before, or ever tried one out.

"You'll need these for your dare," he said, while everyone immediately tested them excitedly. Disappointed, however, they discovered that they didn't work at all. Ox only reacted with a "How stupid do you think I am" look and said:
"Correct. They only work when I say they work. I will only unlock them once you have taken part in the dare. Got it?!" Ox looked over his glasses with a serious expression, making it clear that there was no point in running away with them. Disappointed, Max and Jury agreed, while Finn looked questioning and asked skeptically:
"But there are only two? There are three of us?"
"Don't worry," Ox replied calmly. "I've thought of everything." He reached into the bag again and handed Finn three small trigger chips. They were oval-shaped and made of robust plastic. Ergonomic and perfected in handling. There was a hole in the middle where you could put your finger and activate a switch. The electronics built into them registered every activation. This meant that you could pull the trigger on one of these virtual weapons. The three of them already knew that much. Ox fished a golden coupon out of his backpack.
"You can pick up the third GG at a G-Store," he said. "It's open all day. You must get it activated there and set up your accounts. Only then can you take part in the dare. At six pm it´s starting! Wait, I'll give you the location." Ox pulled out a pen, pulled Finn roughly towards him and scribbled something on his forearm.
"But be damned on time," he mumbled with the pen cap in his mouth. "We can't wait a second longer for you." With that, he packed the bag back into his backpack, threw it over his shoulder and without any hint of goodbye or further explanation, he simply turned around and disappeared into the crowd.

G-Store

The G-Store was nothing more than a kind of designer shop for snobby money monkeys. - Or for those who liked to pretend to be one. - Attention at any price was the motto here. That's why everything in the Store was colorful and flashy. You could buy everything related to Google products here, including one of the GGs. *GG* was the abbreviation for the popular Google Glasses, which had already been use in society for several years. That didn't mean that everyone had a pair of these, after all they still cost a considerable amount, but their functions and features had already become so established that, like the smartphone, people's everyday lives simply couldn't imagine life without them.
So it happened that shortly after the release, the GG was encountered in many everyday situations and it was considered normal for someone to jog and wear distinctive glasses, talk loudly on the phone, or do other things on the net at the same time. However, its initial use through various pop-ups, such as routes, video chats and info buttons, was quickly developed and pushed by the gaming industry. This quickly gave rise to the term *Realgamer*, which would certainly never have found a meaningful use without these glasses. People still remembered the one commercial that changed everything:

Jingle Jingle. The sun is shining, and the birds are chirping. The camera slowly moves through a window into a kitchen. An old woman is draping a cake there. She is humming quietly to herself and carefully positioning white sorbet roses on the exaggerated pink icing. Suddenly a noise. Someone is disturbing the romantic silence. It is the typical noise of an anti-aircraft gun, supported by the assault rifle of the new AK 27 series. The woman's lovely facial expressions immediately escape, and her husband screams from the next room. Apparently, the son has turned up the

console again and the woman feels compelled to act. She marches straight into his room. She wrinkles her nose in disgust. There, between disorganized junk and chaos, her former angel is sitting on a saggy sofa. With tattered dirty laundry, he has blocked out the sunshine and, sweating and straining, he looks at the flickering screen. Despite the door now being open, he does not react, just presses his controller wildly.
"Boy, don't you want to go outside and play? The weather is so nice," the woman calls out between the thunder of a stick grenade.
“Maa no, not today,” replies the boy, tugging at his greasy hair and continuing to play without turning his head towards the door.
“Okay, but at least clean your room.”
“Maybe,” he replies.
"Maybe?! I hear that all the time. Something has to change." She shakes her head. "And I hope that's Nutella on your cheek."
“I think so,” says the boy, wiping his face and demanding that the door be closed.
Scene in the living room while eating cake:
"Hermann, do something," she says with desperation in her voice. "I think the boy is eating his own shit by now." Suddenly the camera pans and someone is standing in the middle of the living room. It is a man in a suit. Well-groomed and the tie has style.
"Who are you and how did you get in?" asks the husband confused. But the camera has long since stopped and only has eyes for the man in the suit, who replies casually:
"Such a nice place and I'm not even offered a coffee?" The camera now goes into a close-up and follows the man every step through the suddenly dilapidated house. He takes a big piece of the woman’s cake, looks mischievously into the camera, and starts hammering out the well-known advertising slogan:
"You finally want to get your son out of the house again? I have just the right thing for you. The new product is called Google

GLASSES. The perfect technology that gives you all the freedom that YOU and everyone out there (he points his finger towards the camera) needs TODAY."
The boy is still sitting and gaming on the sofa. Then the man comes in and puts him on the glasses from behind. The room suddenly looks clean and pure. The man pushes him through the front door of the house. The sun is shining brightly, and everything is green and blooming. The boy who was also confused at first, is now clearly impressed. The man smiles, as do his parents. Finally, the woman lays languishing her head on the unknown man's shoulders. Another medical safety warning, then it's over and *Jingle Jingle* again.

The boys chose the G-Store near the center. Inside there were colorful seat cushions in the familiar Google colors. There was also an elaborate drinks machine that reminded some of a nuclear-powered hyper-sleep cabin. All kinds of varieties were on offer there. From soft drinks, energy and power drinks, vegan milkshakes, to piping hot lifestyle coffee. All at a fairly overpriced price, of course. Right next to it was a snack bar plus an integrated, fully automatic popcorn machine, which also spat out the corn in bright colors. Everything else was kept rather simple and manageable. On the sides there were small, easily visible glass shelves where carefully draped products waited for their new owner. In the middle there was a wide, curved designer counter where a young woman was working. It was only later in the story that the three of them would find out that almost every Realgamer in the city knew her by the name Trixi.
Trixi had two long braids that pointed left and right like a Japan schoolgirl. She also wore elaborate glittery make-up. In Google colors, of course, combined with a bright green lipstick. Her ears were pierced with small prohibition signs and her slender neck was adorned with countless necklaces that made a very special sound with every little movement. Underneath she usually wore a sleeveless top and an equally short denim skirt with sewn-on

glitter stones. Her legs were therefore mainly covered by pulled-up knee socks, which were tucked into high wedge heels. Her step therefore clattered almost threateningly as she strutted from one customer to the next. But this time, as so often, she was standing behind the counter and talking loudly on the phone with a customer. Apparently, he had a complaint on his mind, because while Trixi listened to his concerns more or less attentively with the words:
When she heard "Yeah, yeah, okay?" she chewed a piece of gum in annoyance and her mood became even more annoyed when she saw the new three guys in her store. They had stopped in the entrance in amazement and were now heading purposefully towards her counter.
"Oh no, please. Not these little superfreaks in my store again." she said, as if she had known the three of them for years and knew exactly what they wanted. She did that to everyone. It seemed to be a trend to address complete strangers like an annoying friend. That was a sign of success. And you wouldn't hardly believe it: It worked. The store was buzzing and for this and many other questionable reasons, Trixi could simply allow herself this special kind of customer service. She covered the microphone of her phone with one hand and said:
"I really don't have time for your ridiculous requests. Get out of here. You're driving away all my customers with your rocked down outfits." After this sentence of direct honesty, she turned back to the person on the phone and kept an eye on potential new customers who were buzzing around between the shelves. Trixi could handle several customers at the same time, as long as they left the store with something expensive. That was her undisputed passion and also the reason why she had been able to call this store one of the most successful in the city for years. The customer on the other end of the line had now burst into tears, as was not to overhear, and was sobbing something like "guarantee" and "refund" into the phone. But Trixi stood firm:

"...No, I can't do that. ...No." And with a final word like "impossible" she hung up. Finally, it was time to serve the boys. But Trixi wordlessly pulled a scented spray from under the counter and sprayed it directly into Max's face. He had probably looked at her breasts for too long.
"Didn't I just say something?!" she said to herself. "But you guys welcome to come back tomorrow. When you've had the pleasure of a long and soapy shower." Trixi chewed her gum loudly and made an annoying hand gesture towards the exit.
"But we only wanted to pick up a pair of glasses," Finn said confidently, as Max began to cough terribly under the influence of the lavender scent and Jury generally avoided such questionable situations. But at that moment Trixi had already discovered new fresh meat and immediately rushed towards an older lady who looked like big money.
"You've chosen a very nice model, my favorite gran. It matches you... but... your outfit still needs to be improved," she called out, cutting off Finn's important request. The boys panicked. Without the glasses, they couldn't possibly all take part in the dare. But Finn was not going to let it get that far. He grabbed the coupon and walked towards Trixi and the older lady with a lot of anger in his stomach, who eyeing critically a newly designed GG, decorated with natural stones. Probably freshly imported from some Aztec quarry in central Guatemala.
"A really beautiful model," Finn said to the lady and smiled. "These stones in particular highlight its uniqueness. If I were you, I would take it straight away."
“Oh, what kind of flatterer are you?” she laughed in surprise and looked at herself again in one of the many mirrors.
"You know what?" she said suddenly, exhilarated. "You're absolutely right. That's exactly what I'll take." The lady excitedly turned another mirror to get a better look at herself. Trixi, who hadn't stopped complimenting the woman from all sides until then, looked down at Finn and hissed:
"What in hell do you want?"

Finn pulled out the golden coupon and held it provocatively under her nose. Incredulous, she began to read the stamped inscription in her usual bored manner:
"The owner of this coupon will receive a GG from one of the officially recognized G-Stores." A derogatory "Tizzz" formed between Trixi's bright green lips.
"A well-made fake, my boy. I've never laughed so much." And with these words, she turned back to the old lady. Finn immediately ran after her and never left Trixi's side. The same was true for Jury and Max. They ran excitedly back and forth in front of her counter, begging, arguing, pleading. But for Trixi, this was not an unusual situation at all. She was already familiar with this behavior from many businesspeople. Grown men who would literally fall to their knees just to be given some kind of preferential treatment in some free offer. The old lady had already had her new acquisition wrapped up when the three of them were still waving the coupon and saying something like:
"It's real. Here! It has the unforgeable GG seal," they said. But even when some customers almost left the store disgusted by her pleas, Trixi stood firm.

Time was running out. Ox's words that they should not be late were still echoing in their minds and according to the location he had scribbled on Finn's arm, his meeting point wasn't really around the corner either. The old lady enthusiastically pulled the elaborately packaged GG, plus the designer bag, over the counter and, after Trixi's cash register had let out a cheering beep, strutted towards the exit. As the lady walked past, she paused for a moment and said:
"I wish you luck in redeeming this coupon, but if you don't manage it, here's a little consolation." She pressed a coin into each of their hands and then disappeared behind the passing traffic on the adjacent street. The three of them looked after her, dejected, but when the cars gave a view of the other side again, she had just disappeared.

"So...?" Trixi's voice rang out and held out her hand as if she was demanding the money which was given them from the old lady. The boys hesitated.
"Well, the coupon," she said annoyed and burst an oversized bubble of chewing gum. "I have to have the computer check it first," she explained. Finn looked suspicious, but eventually handed it over. He had no choice. Too much time had passed to go to another store now.

Few customers remained. Only a few who were standing at the popcorn machine, laughing and chatting. Others had disappeared far into the shelves when Trixi changed her mind. The coupon seemed to be more than valid. She wrinkled one of her pierced eyebrows in surprise after she had placed the golden paper under a scanner and took out of a code-protected safe what she called a "demonstration model."
The three of them could hardly believe their luck. Only when Trixi accidentally discovered one of Ox's glasses did they have to listen to a lecture:
"You've been tinkering with the things," she said, "I can see that. It's illegal. You know that." But the boys quickly hid them in their pockets again, as instructive sentences about "warranty void" and the lack of "resale value" flew across the counter. But who cared? They finally had their glasses and excitedly tested some of the basic functions. All other features would gradually become available once their accounts had been set up. Jury, Max and Finn were amazed and argued about who would be allowed to try them out next.
"You have to be careful," she warned, "when you use unauthorized programs. They often have bugs. That's more than dangerous." Apparently, Trixi had fallen into one of her usual sales modes again, so she repeated herself more than once. She set up an account for everyone, downloaded the latest operating system and explained the most basic functions. Until the boys looked at the time in horror and left in a hurry.

"...You really have to be careful," they were heard calling. But the three were already out the door and Trixi looked after them worriedly.

Julius, Admin of Forrester

The street name on Finn's arm had long since been smeared when the boys arrived at the meeting point, rushed but on time. The huge mall of the city center spread out before them. They were standing on one of those typical forecourts. The place where you go from one of the tram stations directly onto a high glass front. But when they looked around, there was no one there. Apart from the hundreds of people, of course, who were experiencing the stressful joys of shopping. No Ox or anyone who identified themselves as a Forrester was to be seen. Max asked a passerby what time it was. But he just pushed him aside in annoyance and disappeared, grumbling to himself, into one of the many tunnel passages that led into the cool underground. The boys ran excitedly through the crowds.

It was strange. Here, in this part of the city that was relatively unknown to the three of them, people seemed to be doing much better. Overstuffed shopping bags hit them from all sides, while they kept a watchful eye on each other. They stopped in front of the mall entrance, a little aside from the crowd streaming in and out. A security guard, who had taken up position just behind the high glass front, looked at them skeptically. Jury seemed somehow familiar to him, but that was of no interest at that moment. Because where were the Forresters? That was the question that each of the boys asked themselves with a puzzled expression. Because according to Jury's sense of time, which the others thought was the most precise, it must already be shortly before six. And how were they supposed to find each other here, among all these people?
"Couldn't they have found a better meeting point? This is madness," complained Max. The minutes passed. Had they perhaps got the location wrong? After all, Ox's scribble had been difficult to decipher, and it was now too late to check the street

name again. Finn's arm was now just a black, greasy stain due to sweat. They looked at each other in outrage. Jury, on the other hand, pulled his GG out of his trouser pocket and put it on. When Max and Finn noticed this, they also took out their glasses and each of them immediately made an astonished face. In the meantime, the glasses had activated themselves and logged in unnoticed. All features and functions had now been downloaded and as soon as the boys looked through their GGs, the cityscape suddenly changed.

Whole building facades, which initially seemed tired and dreary, suddenly shone with a completely new splendor. A splendor that you first had to find the right words for. In the glass wall of the mall, for example, brightly animated advertising clips were shown. Now and then the actors even floated over them and greeted the new customers. Advertising banners and flickering fonts as far as the eye could see. Footpaths where cars were constantly crossing lit up in flashing colors and as soon as one of the traffic lights turned red, you were shown a new, green-marked path on the floor that led you safely through the maze of streets. There even seemed to be a virtual bus stop here and at a Chinese takeaway, the name was immediately translated and displayed in the appropriate style. Even on the forecourt of the mall, real artists were apparently having fun. They used holo effects to create famous paintings and strange installations that you could even interact with. The boys were amazed and showed and tried out everything that the new wonder world had to offer them. Yes, technology had obviously made another huge leap forward that was simply hidden from people without this device.

Among the countless colorful lights, strangely dressed people could also be seen. In fact, some of them seemed to be wearing some kind of virtual decoration or accessory on their clothing. There were hair and head ornaments, moving tattoos on the skin, or a protruding watch on the jacket.

But two figures in particular caught the boys' attention. They were walking straight towards them in the middle of the crowd. Their sight was more than unusual. As strange as it may sound, they were wearing a kind of armor. One that shone in magnificent colors, just like the advertisements. Their faces were covered by shiny helmets. One was slim and flat, so that it resembled that of a futuristic astronaut. The other had small horned spikes above a wide protective visor that shone bronze and looked like a Roman soldier's helmet, which formed something like a mohawk over the head. Their arms and legs were armored by various parts that came together to form a whole in an almost mystical way.
This sight left everyone speechless. But strangely enough, the people walking by didn't seem to notice. They pushed past the colorful figures and hurried on their way.
The striking armor was obviously a typical GG illusion and could only be seen by those who wore such glasses. GG had the special feature of not only displaying a virtual reality, but also showing normal reality like conventional glasses. But it was provided with small, more or less helpful overlays. But this was more than just a simple overlay, and even the boys who had never seen anything similar before understood that. Only Max said that he had once read something about virtual clothing. But these outfits exceeded even his often-vivid imagination.
Suddenly Finn noticed that these two strange figures were getting closer and closer and in just a few steps they approached the boys. Finn was just about to make room, but they just stopped and apparently looked at him. It was impossible to read their looks under their helmets, but after a short moment it seemed as if they were actually waiting for the boys, here among all the people. The three of them looked at each other, visibly surprised, until one of the figures said something:
"So..., these are the Stationgamers," was heard in a critical tone. His counterpart raised a hand to his temple and suddenly the helmet opened in a spectacular way. Faint lines were first drawn

through its initially smooth shape. At first, they were narrow and then became wider and wider. It only took a moment until everything dissolved into small metallic structures that burst apart noisily. And bit by bit, they revealed a face underneath. Jury, Max and Finn were amazed. It was Ox who was now looking at them expectantly.

What a spectacular appearance, thought Jury, and couldn´t take his eyes off the virtual armor. Because now that it was so close to him, even more ingenious details could be seen. For example, small glowing gizmos lit up in a bluish, translucent light. At regular intervals, they detached themselves from his armor to look for a new place to stay somewhere else, similar to a small crawling creature. But that wasn't all. Ox wore a golden symbol on his chest. A crest that moved gently in the wind like a flag. It was the symbol of the Forrester. The other had a metallic silver armor with drawn chest and abdominal muscles on it, so that one immediately had the image of a Roman centurion in mind.
Jury was so fascinated that he had to shake himself to listen to what the two of them were saying. Ox introduced his counterpart in an unusually formal manner, while he took off his helmet just as spectacularly.
"May I introduce," he said with an almost majestic bow. "Julius, Admin of the Forrester."

Under the helmet was a surprisingly young face. Perhaps just a year or two older than the boys. With blond hair, similar to Jury's, only a little longer, which is why it kept falling over his face. Underneath was a narrow chin, where a mischievous smile sat. His eyes were slightly covered by the GG, but through them he examined each of the three closely. In greeting, he held out his hand without saying a word. Only now did you notice that his own hand disappeared into the large glove of his armor. Max kept taking off his GG to distinguish what was real and what was fake. Meanwhile, Jury was still marveling at Ox's little gizmos.

Even when you got closer to them, they made a slightly whispering, even humming sound. The armor was obviously linked to his own glasses. On each side, it had an ear stud built into a flexible strap. This could not only transmit the usual ambient noises to the ear, but also play its own sounds. That was how the sound had to work, he thought.
"So? Are you ready?" Julius interrupted his thoughts. The boys nodded tensely.
“I hope you have everything you need with you?” Ox asked critically, checking the new glasses from the G-Store.
"It was a good idea to let the Stationgamers show up half an hour earlier," said Julius, making it clear that the three of them still had some time despite their slight delay. He and Ox prepared to leave the place again.
"What about the dare?" Finn and Max immediately wanted to know.
“Just calm down,” Julius said, waving everyone over and explaining that they were just going to the next parking garage to discuss everything else there.
In contrast to them, Julius remained calm and seemed to be amused that people were still admiring his armor. The illusion was too perfect. Even movements were imitated and adapted without any problem. Jury, who had fallen behind a little, kept taking off his glasses, just like Max, to be able to determine the difference between reality and virtual exaggeration more precisely. The fascination left neither him nor his friends. Clearly, this sight was more than unusual, "extreme" was perhaps the better word here, but despite the almost dreamlike appearance of Ox and Julius the admin, it was surprisingly familiar to the boys. Because after a moment's thought, Jury remembered: Yes, of course, that was definitely INFINITY.

After a few minutes' walk, they came to a multi-story parking garage. It was surprisingly empty, and it was only when Ox pointed to a large sign that said "*dilapidated*" that they

understood why. There were only a few isolated cars parked there and wild graffiti and dumped garbage on the weathered walls, and between the barrier tapes, poor repair work had obviously begun. At least a few bags of cement and building rubble were evidence of this. And here, in this run-down place, a test of courage was supposed to take place? That seemed more than unusual, and not just to Jury. Even Max and Finn looked just as questioning, so that Julius immediately jumped in between their skepticism:
"You're surprised, aren't you? Have you ever played Infinity in a parking garage?" All three answered the question with a collective shake of their heads and then he started to explain.

As a Realgamer, there was obviously a lot to consider. Each of the boys was surprised to discover this. While Ox examined the weapons, they had brought with them and checked their trigger ships for sufficient stability and strength, Julius explained that the graffiti was not just trivial scribbles. Realgamers used certain signs and symbols to mark the entrance to a level. This entrance was marked by three diagonal lines with a horizontal line underneath. If it was a time-limited level or event, the start time and duration could be determined by adding numbers.
Julius pulled out a small spray bottle and used red paint to complete the narrow contours of one of the symbols he had explained on a wall in the parking garage. He also added a new start time and some cryptic symbol. But Jury still didn't quite understand how you could play a shooter in the middle of a parking garage. Let alone how a level entrance opened up on a solid concrete wall. But he wasn't the only one plagued by such questions. But Julius spoke with each passing minute a little faster. After all, there were basic things, as he emphasized, that Realgamers had to pay unconditional attention to.
You should only follow the indicated paths and generally give a wide berth to chasms. Furthermore, there could sometimes be bugs that were only dangerous if you left your position during

them. A basic feeling for *real* and *unreal* would also be good. Communication with your teammates took place via a subprogram called VC, which simply meant voice connect and enabled you to talk to each other even over long distances. Stationgamers called it team speak and was basically the same thing.
Julius talked and talked. But now, so close to the dare, the boys were a bit overwhelmed by the amount of information, which raised more questions than it answered. In addition, they were constantly distracted by new things, which made it almost impossible to concentrate on listening. They were much more amazed by the representation of their weapons. After a somewhat complicated software activation by Ox, which transformed in a fantastic way. When looking through the glasses, Jury's screwed-together frame with handle became a futuristic-looking rapid-fire weapon, which consisted of an elongated shaft and snow-white armor plates. Max, on the other hand, euphorically described his as a double-barreled scout rifle, where you could obviously also fire grenades from the lower barrel. Finn got one of those modern laser rifles that had nothing in common with reality. They were pure fantasy weapons that fired a kind of laser or plasma beam with a loud roar through a magnetized barrel and thus looked extremely stylish. That's why Jury and Max were amazed when Finn fired a test shot at the ceiling of the parking space and small white-hot plasma balls formed there, which then even dripped from the ceiling with a quiet hissing sound.
"Your weapons are low level to begin with," Ox apologized, almost inappropriately, "But you don't get anything for free here either. So, you'll have to make do with that for now," he said. The boys nodded taciturnly because they were more than satisfied. Excited, they kept looking through their visors and looking for targets that they could shoot at. Funnily enough, every impact of their projectiles always left a damage or burn mark, without literally doing anything. All three then took turns taking off their

glasses to check whether what was actually the case, and after they had played through this scenario several times, they never stopped looking for a new target. They laughed and joked, and shortly thereafter even shot at themselves. This went on until Ox looked annoyed to Julius, where he spoke again:
"Maybe you should have told them that their ammo is limited," he said, so the three immediately stopped firing and from then on listened intently to what he had to say.
"In this stage you will have to deal with Grudges," Julius said. "As soon as it opens, you should reach out for a safe place to check the situation. Because grudges - as you hopefully know - are not to be trifled with." Julius words echoed through the parking garage and the three of them remembered their countless fights with these creatures.
Grudges were animal creatures. They moved mainly on all fours and were known for their long and high jumps. They got their name from the deafening roar they let out from their dark and toothed throats before each attack. Clawed paws would then strike at you and if you didn't kill them right away, you really had nothing to laugh about. Julius continued:
"And now for the important part," he said, "One of the Grudges looks a little different than the others. What it is exactly, we cannot say. It is always a different detail that is changed. This particular grudge carries a key. You must kill it to get it. Bring me the key and you will be accepted into the Forresters. It is as simple as that."
The boys nodded and immediately put their heads together. They discussed who should position themselves where with which weapon, what was strange because no one had any idea what to expect. Everyone counted their ammunition again until Julius and Ox reminded them that time was running out and suddenly said goodbye to the boys.
“Wait?” Finn said incredulously, “Aren’t you guys at the fight?!”
"No, no," Julius waved off, "From now on, you're on your own. Just bring me this key. We'll wait for you guys until it`s finished."

"All you have to do is scan the sign," said Ox, "and at the right time the checkpoint will activate." With these few and simple words, they both left the parking garage and left the boys alone.

The dare

The three of them stared spellbound through their GGs. After scanning the graffiti that Julius had sprayed on the wall, a countdown appeared. The seconds there hurried down incessantly. Nobody said anything. Only Max, who usually always had a light-hearted joke on his lips, started to stutter. That was just how he was when he got nervous. That's why we didn't hear anything from him shortly afterwards and with every new second that came closer, the three friends moved closer together. Just before the countdown reached zero, a woman's voice was heard. And as if the tension wasn't enough, she threateningly counted down the very last seconds:
"Event starts in five seconds! Five...four...three...two...ONE!"

Another scan was now carried out before their eyes. Shallow, thin white lines were drawn over the graffiti until it began to flash several times. Then the lines continued. Over the floor, ceiling, pillars, cars and finally over everything else that was there in the parking garage. Only now did thin overdrawing's in a polygon structure become activated, step by step, transforming the oh-so-grey floor into the floor of a stony cave. The otherwise desolate concrete pillars became mystical stalactites. Ones that slowly and growingly clung to the pillars. In the light, which soon became increasingly shallow, they shimmered in greenish-grey colors. The few cars that had been left there turned into rough rock formations, with small, delicate ferns growing at the bottom. The equally grey walls had, only a moment later, given way to a spacious rock structure, in the gaps and cracks of which streams of water were forming.

The three of them couldn't believe their eyes. This ordinary parking garage had just turned into a fantastic cave world in just few seconds. Unbelievable. Jury and Max would have loved to run off straight away to explore everything, but Finn held them back resolutely. He quickly ducked behind a boulder, which was actually a dented VW-bus, and pointed with his finger to a shady spot where, after looking for a while, something seemed to be moving. Jury and Max now remembered Julius' words to check the situation first before going inside the stage. It didn't take long before the two of them also looked for a safe place to stay behind the fern bushes. They looked over more rocks and searched the area for possible dangers. But after staying in a crouched position for a while, Jury couldn't take it anymore. He freed himself from Max's spontaneous shoulder grip, stepped into the middle of the cave and bravely went forward.

Each step made a crunching, unmistakable sound, so Jury fearfully drew his weapon and cautiously continued on. The others looked after him uncertainly, but then decided to do the same and secure the left and right sides. Just as they were used to do as Stationgamers.

Jury cast a quick glance back over his shoulder and then continued on with a little more courage. He fixed his eyes on a spot that he thought was a good vantage point. In the middle of the cave, a high rock stood out from a hazy cone of light. From there, you would certainly have a good view, and whatever dark creature was lurking between these rocks, Jury knew one thing for sure: Like all evil creatures, they avoid the light. Therefore, he didn't hesitate and walked a little faster towards it and, as if he had already suspected it, at that moment a mighty monster shot out of the shadow. Jury caught his breath. He had fought these creatures' countless times as a Stationgamer, but what he saw now made his knees shake.

A grudge almost as big as a school bus. His skin was scaly and wet. Gray fur grew across his humped back, where pointed horns stood up at the end of his shoulder. The long claws on his paws dug into the ground in front of him. His nostrils breathed deeply and strongly. Small, spoon-like ears stood up. His scaly tail snaked menacingly over the ground.

This Grudge not only looked damn real but acted like it too. He stared at Jury with emerald green eyes. He practically stared at him, bared his teeth, and stamped his feet. Jury didn't move. He couldn't. Hiding was pointless now. He drew his weapon reflexively. The Grudge hurled deafening roars and strings of spit at him until he ran straight at Jury. His speed frightening. His paws the size of plates. Jury fired. Lightning-like bullets shot across the cave. The Grudge raged and deflected the bullets with his horned skull while he headed purposefully towards Jury. Suddenly projectiles flew from the sides. The Grudge staggered, but quickly pulled himself up again, because Jury was only a few steps away. Suddenly Jury had to reload. But how did you do that as a Realgamer? How could one reload a weapon that was actually just a tubular frame made of rusty scrap parts?
Jury repeatedly grabbed at nothing. A magazine reload was displayed on his weapon, but it was no use. The Grudge came closer and at the same moment prepared to make a mighty leap. Jury took a few clumsy steps backwards until the Grudge thundered down on him. Shots flew through the air and hit at the very last moment, so that the Grudge felt lifeless and lay dead in front of Jury with its tongue hanging out.
"Pulse bullets," said Max calmly. After emerging from one of the dark corners in a similar way to Grudge and grinning at Jury, he said, "They reload automatically after every hit."
"Ha..ha," Jury snapped back. "That.. was.. NOT funny," he said.
"You could tell," Finn joined in, laughing. Apparently the two of them had listened to this part of Julius' never-ending speech and knew how to reload a virtual weapon. It was actually quite simple, Finn explained. You either had to press a virtual button on the weapon, which lit up wildly when the magazine was empty, or simply hold down the trigger for some time.
“Maybe he should have listened a little better,” they joked, while Jury just marveled at the dead resentment.

The Grudge lay there lifeless. Its small, wrinkled eyes remained closed. The others also approached now, but they remained cautious. Because all too often one of these creatures would simply rear up again and thrash around even more wildly than before, roaring loudly. But this one did not move at all. The four powerful paws were stretched out in front of him. Its skull was covered with deep scars, the skin wrinkled and thick. The boys were amazed at the details that made the creature seem incredibly real. But there were only seconds before the Grudge literally vanished into thin air before them.
"The key? Where is the key?" Finn was heard saying and everyone looked around again. There had to be more of these creatures around. They all agreed on that. So, they continued determinedly. Deeper and deeper into the branching corridors that were in the real-world paths for cars, customers, and people. This time Finn went first, and Max and Jury followed him.

Complete beginners

Finn generally trusted his quick comprehension when hunting. He relied on his sharp eyes and his equally sharp mind. Jury was more of a quick reactor, but also a tactician. He was always looking for a good position from which he might have some advantages or be able to take an opponent under fire. Max, on the other hand, was guided solely by his instincts. Sometimes it worked surprisingly well, sometimes not at all. It mostly depended on his mood. But despite all that, he acted more as a motivator, who could bring down every obstacle with a casual saying. At least that was his very own theory.

It wasn't long before footprints, slimy rocks and suspicious grunting noises revealed the presence of more Grudges. They were scurrying around behind shadows deep in the cave. This time it was no problem for the boys to take them down one by one. With every well-aimed shot and hit they became more confident and more enthusiastic about the hunt.
"You'll have it in a minute!" was heard between the roar of thundering projectiles. The deep roar of the Grudges, which leapt wildly over rocks and opened their mouths wide to attack, also filled the room. But with every dead animal that sank motionless to the ground, the three wondered where the one with the key was.
It was only later that a small, reserved Grudge with orange fur on its back appeared among the turmoil. When Finn saw it, it was immediately clear: It had to be it. This Grudge must carry the key. He immediately called the others over and pointed to a rock where it was cleverly hidden behind ferns and dark shadows. Jury fired a few well-aimed shots. But the Grudge just hopped over them and jumped in long leaps into a hiding place opposite.
"That's unbelievable how fast it is." Finn was not the only one to wonder. Max and Jury also failed in their attempt to catch it.

Thus, the three followed the Grudge to the end of the cave, where it had run into a corridor and the beautiful rock formations suddenly stopped. The stone-grey concrete floor was revealed again. Heating pipes hung from the ceiling and even the cars now showed their real shape again. At the end of the corridor, they had stepped back into the real world. The game was clearly over here, but the Grudge continued running regardless. It didn't care about parked cars or an old elevator shaft, which it quickly slipped into and sprinted up to the busy shopping center. The three of them couldn't believe their eyes. They ran after the Grudge as best they could. They followed it up a staircase to the entrance of the mall, where they could see the typical glass front. The grudge jumped back and forth between the people and even skillfully avoided a few crowds. Then it passed the countless shops until it finally disappeared somewhere in the tumult of costumers.

Surprised, the boys crouched down behind a few garbage cans not far from the entrance and thought about what they could do now. After all, you couldn't just run around among the people with a homemade weapon and shoot at some imaginary monster. That would inevitably attract attention. The boys were aware of that, so they were still sitting closely packed behind the cans and discussing wildly. Was this perhaps a glitch? And what if it wasn't? How should you defeat a grudge that just left the game whenever it wanted? Would Julius take them in without a key? All questions that were flying around wildly and this time it was Finn who had had enough after an uncomfortable while. He didn’t want to step in front of the Forresters without this key. This would have been much more embarrassing for him than just slipping into a mall and taking care of a small Grudge, he complained. So, he didn't ask his friends for permission, but pulled himself together and ran straight towards the entrance. His friends looked after him, somewhat horrified. Finn moved in a zigzag through the crowd, always in such way that a direct view was blocked. He made it to the entrance without any problem. Because the busy customers obviously had more important things to do than to worry about a boy with ar-glasses, a worn-out hoodie, and an indefinable spring frame in his hand. When he arrived at the security staff, this was more difficult. But here too, Finn took advantage of a group of shoppers, with whom he slipped through the wide door in a crouched position. After Max and Jury had observed the scene from a safe distance, it was now their turn. They didn't think twice and just as skillfully followed Finn into the entrance hall of the mall.

A glass dome adorned the spacious, high ceiling, from where daylight mixed with the magnificent lamps. In the main hall there were large escalators that transported people from one level to another. Large screens lit up everywhere, advertising new products. Behind them were well-decorated glass fronts with mannequins in everyday poses and hip clothes. And somewhere in between were some boys with torn clothes and dirty faces, with a GG on their head, straining to look for something.

The Grudge had mingled with the crowd and was trying to avoid them. Finn fired a few accurate shots and hit them. But that was apparently not enough to kill, because the Grudge again skillfully jumped over benches and a decorative fountain and disappeared shortly afterwards, once again in the fray. In the meantime, Jury had taken a different route. He had somewhat involuntarily gone up one of the many escalators with the crowd. From there he had a good view of what was happening, because after Finn fired a few shots at the Grudge, Jury had aimed at him from above and watched closely where it disappeared to.
Truly it was strange. None of the people reacted to the loud bullets or were frightened by the sight of that Grudge charging towards them, baring his teeth. Of course, only someone who was wearing Google glasses like the guys and was also in the game could see it, but it was still strange to watch.

Jury was looking tensely through the virtual visor and clutching his weapon, which was now fully reloaded. He aimed at the unsuspecting crowd. You would think an assassin had mingled with them, but it was just a boy playing a game. He was targeting a Grudge in order to land a single, fatal blow. Down there, near the escalator, he was creeping around, grunting, and avoiding any contact with the people crossing the mall. He skillfully dodged them again and again.
"How does that work?" Jury asked himself. But before he could finish his thought, he suddenly saw a conspicuous man running into the scene. It was the security guard from the main entrance. Apparently, he had noticed something because he immediately looked up at Jury. Right through his visor. Then back to the place where the Grudge was romping about and shouted:
“HEY YOU! This isn’t a playground for gamers!”
Jury immediately starts to run and disappeared from the guard's vision as quickly as he could. He ran in a wide arc on the upper floor so that he could still keep an eye on the Grudge and avoid the man who was keeping order and security in the mall as much as possible. But suddenly more people blocked his view and when Jury looked back at the Grudge's location, he had disappeared. Jury was convinced that he only needed a few more targeted hits, and he was determined to get them in before it was too late.
The security guard, however, did not disappear so easily. Unfortunately, he did not let up and started to pursue him. Jury rushed through the now increasingly narrow alleys of people. He banged into bags and protruding elbows. Some looked up indignantly, others complained and cursed loudly. But Jury kept running, strenuously. Always in the direction he thought the Grudge was going. The security guard followed him, because his bunch of keys began to ring more and more clearly. But Jury did not let himself be distracted from his goal. The Grudge was more important now and the only thing that really concerned him. Suddenly, out of nowhere, shots flew past. Jury recognized Finn's

plasma bullets. He had obviously fired at the Grudge. And indeed, at the end of the path, where two escalators went up in the middle of the mall, Finn and Max had cornered him. He defended himself there with almost frightened sounds and Jury immediately set about getting a final headshot. Easier said than done because the Grudge kept shooting out of his now red-glowing target. Without thinking twice, Jury fired two shots in quick succession between the people and suddenly the Grudge collapsed at the foot of the escalator without any further resistance. Then he immediately dissolved into thin air and at the place where all movement had left his body, a small golden pyramid popped out. It fell to the ground with a loud clinking sound. It had to be it. The key!

Jury, Max, and Finn cheered. They raised their weapons and celebrated their victory despite the crowd. Jury immediately ran to get the key. But suddenly he noticed a man, the sight of whom made Finn and Max flee in a flash. It was the security guard, who was coming slowly towards him on the escalator directly opposite.
"Didn't I warn you?!" he said in a commanding tone and pointed at Jury with a finger that seemed to pierce him like an arrowhead.
"No GAMERS in MY mall," he hissed through his teeth, taking a deep, heavy breath. The man had reached the foot of the escalator, his eyes fixed on Jury. The golden pyramid was only a few steps ahead of him. Jury would have grabbed the little something long ago, but since he didn't know how to take a virtual item, he hesitated. And it was precisely this hesitation that had now caused valuable seconds to pass. Because how long would it stay there? Jury was undoubtedly a complete beginner in realgaming, but if there was one thing he knew for sure, it was that he didn't have much time left. He approached the security guard uncertainly, putting on a chastened expression. Because right at his feet, the little pyramid sparkled. The key that they had

promised Julius and would only allow them to join the Forrester clan.
Jury therefore stepped closer and made it clear with a dejected attitude that he was ready to accept his punishment. Again and again, he let his gaze wander to the floor. There it was still lying. And when the security guard reached out his hand to him, he quickly ducked under it and slid across the floor towards the key. But the security guard was faster. With a precise move he grabbed Jury by the collar and dragged him into an office at the end of a long dark corridor.

Waste of time

The security guard was pissed off. Too bad that Jury didn't notice at that time that he had caught the pyramid after all. Because before the security guard could press the off button on the GG and throw it in his desk drawer in frustration, it was already put in his inventory list.

Jury had to answer annoying questions behind a sloppy desk and between the hum of a smelly air condition:

"Parents?" said the tall man in a serious and rough tone of voice, staring at his screen and getting ready to enter a name into the system.

"I don't have any," Jury answered defiantly, but this confidence vanished when the security guard looked at him with a piercingly skeptical look. As if he already knew that this was a lie. The man took a deep breath, reached for a sandwich that had been left lying around and looked down at Jury with exaggerated smacking noises:

"I see. So, you don't have any," he said, tearing another large piece out of the already battered bread, so that parts of it clattered dully onto the table.

"Listen, buddy," he said. "I know exactly when I'm being fooled." And as he leaned deeply into the worn-out office chair, a few bites disappeared into his mighty gullet. Despite the disgusting eating noises, Jury noticed how hungry he was. But the man continued to eat greedily and without stopping and pointed to a large sign hanging on the wall behind him. In bold letters and in the best and harshest official speak, there was a long, never-ending text.

“Read aloud,” he ordered, and Jury obeyed.

“DUE TO THEIR OWN SAFETY REASONS, OUR CUSTOMERS ARE PROHIBITED FROM WEARING VIRTUAL GLASSES OR SIMILAR PRODUCTS, IN GENERAL AND WITHOUT EXCEPTION, INSIDE THESE BUILDING” Jury paused.

"... WITHOUT EXCEPTION," the man yelled the words. "Do you understand what that means?" he shouted, so that spit and the remains of a tomato flew into Jury's face. He wiped his cheek and thought about what Finn or Max would do in this situation. But he didn't want to sing a song about useless safety reasons either.
“But... but I’m not a customer,” he said sheepishly.
"Bro," the man widened his eyes and waved the sandwich so that some dip flew across the table. "You think you're super smart, don't you?" The security guard took another breath, held his chest to check that his heart hadn't jumped out of its socket, and used a dropped pin to sort out some of the notes that had been pinned up behind his back. One of them showed footage from a surveillance camera. Clear faces that, judging by the heading *BANNED OUT*, all had something to do with realgaming. Jury even recognized Julius and Ox's faces and concluded that this was not the first attempt to kill a grudge in this mall.
After a few concentrated breathing exercises, the security guard calmed down again, and the typical sentences of an adult followed:
What is the point of playing around anyway? I don't understand how anyone can waste their time like that. Is it getting you anywhere? What would your parents say? Go to school. Make something of yourself. Think about your future. What will become of you? Take an example from others. Your friends are nothing more than fools, idlers, and strayers and so on.
At the end of the lecture, which mainly consisted of sentences like: "Gaming is a waste of time", there was the obligatory ban from the premises and the confiscation of the allegedly unauthorized GG. But before the security could make another attempt to locate Jury's parents by using the computer, a theft alarm suddenly sounded. Despite his fullness, he jumped up in surprise. He slapped the rest of his snack back on the table in annoyance and ordered Jury not to move from the spot. He closed the door behind him and, with his keys jingling loudly, ran out into the hallway to check that everything was in order.

Admittedly, Jury had fibbed a little. Almost more greedily than the security guard, he grabbed his sandwich and thought about it. His parents were probably looking for him and had already pinned or uploaded his photo somewhere, along with a detailed description of what he left the house with.
A violent argument was the trigger that one day caused him to finally leave his tiny room, the dreary terraced house, and the narrow street, with everything that was so familiar to him. It didn't matter what the constantly recurring argument was about. For some time now, his parents had been demanding more and more from him. And the more often they argued, the stronger an unconscious thought grew in him.
Everyone has probably thought about it at some point: What if I suddenly disappear? What would they do then? And with hate-filled thoughts you say to yourself: It's their own fault. Their brought this on and now it's too late.
That's why he thought about running away. At first it was just a thought, a little game in his head. But with every new argument, this tender something grew unnoticed. He liked the idea of how sad everyone would be. Finally, they would really worry and understand how stupid their constant demands were. He just wanted to get back at them. Teach them a lesson, and that only worked out if he didn't come back after a few days of absence. And certainly not with a smile on his lips and his arms wide open for a hug. No, he didn't want to make it that easy for them. So it happened that Jury had secretly stowed a few things and even a train ticket in his bed box. The next big city was his destination. And then, one quite morning, he literally set off.

Suddenly the door clicked, but strangely, no one entered. Someone was tampering with it. The handle kept moving from right to left. Shortly afterwards, it opened, but it wasn't the security guard who pushed his head through the gap. It was Max with a mischievous smile:

"Be quiet," he said hastily beckoned Jury over. Jury didn't ask questions. He just grabbed his GG from the fortunately unlocked drawer and ran to the door. Then they both made a quiet getaway.
That was the advantage of having idlers and strayers as friends, thought Jury, because they really knew all kinds of tricks to sneak out of bad places.

Arrival

Jury, Max, and Finn sat exhausted by a fire. Quiet and soothing, it gave off a comforting warmth. The fire pit, however, was located in the middle of a strange space that could hardly be described in simple words.
Snow-white columns could be seen there. Columns with sweeping lines and numerous ornaments. They reached from the floor to a magnificent high ceiling. The columns were arranged in a circle, forming a wide ring around the center. A center, where the fire burned richly in an equally richly decorated silver chalice, were long benches arranged on white marble, on which the three sat and gazed around in amazement. But they couldn't stay in their seats for long. What they discovered everywhere was just too fantastic.

Colorful pennants fluttered from the pillars. In deep red, a multifaceted green, and a velvety sky blue, they reached far up to the vaulted ceiling, which, like the pillars, shimmered with a marble white and had a distinctly Roman or Greek style. Behind it were wide, high walls that made the room seem endless. They were decorated with countless banners and coats of arms. But pictures and even selfies could also be found there. In pairs or with others, one stood before an impressive backdrop. A huge waterfall, for example, and in front of it, in a ravine of meadow grass, lay a slain monster. It looked like a giant insect, with claw-like prehensile teeth. Its head and antennae were lowered, its legs stretched out wide, and as if in a successful hunt, the rangers posed there and made one or two victory gestures in front of their prey.
Not far away, additional trophies had been set up. There were oddly shaped glass containers with strange creatures inside. They were displayed in a random arrangement. Some of them were actually still alive and would thrash around wildly if you just

touched their glass. Others appeared to be dead or petrified. Then they just swam quietly and peacefully, in a torrent of bubbling bubbles. Some were small and cute and even quite pretty to look at. They were reminiscent of elf-like mythical creatures and shimmered in the most vibrant colors. Others were just plain ugly and seemed to have come straight from hell or a horror movie. Because upon closer inspection, you could see a convulsing monster or even something more likely to be described as a mummified alien.
At the end of the wide room was a tall door. Tendrils of golden maple leaves snaked up there, forming an ornate entrance with twisted branches. But as soon as one even approached it, the leaves and twigs began to grow wildly, blocking the way. And that wasn't all. Suddenly, a futuristic object came flying down from somewhere. It looked like a polished egg, with small short wings and black button eyes that could open and close. It performed a kind of scan of the boys and, in a croaking robotic voice, vehemently demanded their identification. When none of them complied, a beeping alarm suddenly went off.
"Turn it off!" someone shouted, while they nonsensically pressed their hands over their ears and looked helpless. Only Julius managed to shut it off again with a, "It's okay. They're my friends." And the little thing, which was probably some kind of surveillance drone, retracted its eyes and wings with an angry sound and floated off in a flash back to where it came from.

The three had successfully passed the test of courage, and everyone was visibly surprised when Ox checked Jury's inventory and found the desired golden pyramid. Overjoyed, the boys accepted the invitation to come to the Forrester headquarters. The two proudly showed them around and told them about their countless adventures at Infinity. Everyone listened to them with rapt attention, each letting their gaze wander over the new, strange, and fantastic things that could be seen in every corner.

For example, tiny cars were racing. With squealing tires, they shot through equally tiny streets that looked completely real, with glowing streetlights, busy intersections, and rows of houses. Even dwarfish pedestrians jumped aside at the sight of the speeding speedsters and shortly thereafter went on their way in a huff.
There was also something resembling an armory. In homemade holders glowing green, one could see bizarre structures that left Jury and Finn guessing what exactly they were. Right next to it lay a variety of sports equipment. Max marveled at a skateboard with flames in changing neon colors blazing from its tires.
"Wow, a VIRTUAL board?! But how is that supposed to work?" he exclaimed excitedly, immediately placing one foot on it. At the same moment, it shot up right away, sending him tumbling backward to the ground in a spectacular move.
“No, that one is real,” said Ox mockingly, and Julius offered him a hand to help him stand up again.
"Yes, we just virtually pimped up the design," he explained, and Max rubbed his aching back in wonder. Because this room, with all its countless things, was even stranger than anything one could have imagined. Here, familiar fantasy stories mingled with cheap action and science fiction movies. Any adult would probably say: This room was neither one thing nor the other. But for the three friends, it was just perfection down to the last detail.

A little later, Max's eyes started to hurt, so he kept taking off his glasses. He didn't like the way they made you sweat after wearing them for a while. And while Jury and Finn once again marveled at the incredible collection of weapons, he leaned a little way off against an old wardrobe that had apparently been left to rot under one of the high windows.
“Watch out,” ranted Ox immediately pulled Max out of his position. Max raised his hands in a placating gesture and said: “It’s just an old cupboard.”

"You might think so," Ox countered, making a move to please put his GG back on. This old wardrobe was actually another one of Forrester's trophy collections. Made of glass, gold, and purple, it also contained strange structures and figures. Some of them even rotated. A kind of bird with outstretched wings, studded with sparkling gemstones, could be seen there, and Ox recounted in a euphoric voice where he had found this special something. "In the Valley of Dreams, there by the secret fortress of Level 6." he said. But Jury and Finn didn't quite understand it either. This trophy cabinet was not a purely virtual creation, but a combination of real ones, and if you shook it, some of them even threatened to fall out. Apparently, virtual content could be linked to real things in such a way that it seemed completely real and even followed conventional physics.
Therefore, it was really difficult, if not impossible, to distinguish the real from the fake in this place and if you weren't careful, you could possibly even cause unrest among the Realgamers.

Finn also learned that in this social hub, as some called the middle and larger part of the headquarters, it didn't make much sense to take off his glasses without a good reason. Because, as he was about to rest on one of the benches near the fire, which was thankfully real, a squeaky voice interrupted:
“Careful! Don’t sit there!”
Amazingly, it was a small boy, probably not even eight years old, who was tumbling around between the fireplace and the benches. Before Finn's rear end even touched the seat, he came running up and shooed something in front of him. Only after Finn put his GG back on did he reveal it to be a small, shaggy puppy. Just like the boy, he was romping around between the benches and, except for the fact that his paws occasionally sank into the ground, his movements and gestures were quite similar to those of a real dog. Finn laughed enthusiastically, while Ox just complained about his mediocre programming.

"That thing's so buggy," he whispered, and proved it by throwing it a real ball, which simply zipped right through him without any reaction. Yes, even as a newbie in realgaming, you had to get used to things like that.

Shortly afterwards, the room filled with other members that Julius and Ox had called together. But the initial conversations with the *newcomers*, as they called them, were rather tentative. The Forresters much preferred to play hoops with a strange basketball. Ox explained that it wasn't a real one, but actually a purely virtual construct. Only the hoop was real. They called it *Pukeball*, and before anyone could even ask why, everything quickly became clear.
One of the guys took a gallant shot, and as soon as the ball flew through the basket, he transformed into a green, slimy, round man. With two short arms, he held onto the rim of the basket, swinging and grinning, and in the voice of a chain smoker, he shouted filthy:
"You're all losers. LOSERS ARE YOU." Then he fell to the ground like a ripe grape and vomited spectacularly in poisonous green goo all over the court. One of the Forresters then grabbed the little guy and he transformed back into a normal basketball again and the game continued. Jury, Max and Finn watched enthusiastically until the others encouraged them to join in. But it was difficult to catch and chase after a ball that didn't actually exist. So, after just a few rounds they ended up sitting tired and exhausted on the benches by the fire. Out of curiosity, they asked a few questions, but the conversation never really got going. But topics like Infinity stats or the rank of their corresponding character were always a good way to lighten the mood.
Only one person broke the recurring silence. It was the little boy with his playful dog, whom everyone called *Little Tony*. He wore a shapka pulled low over his face, one of those old-fashioned aviator caps with flapping ears on either side. Whether intentionally or unintentionally, he looked very similar to his

virtual pet. Because even the ears of Tony's cap flapped back and forth with every movement like his dog, who, despite the poor AI, was constantly looking for something to eat. So that Little Tony frantically stuffed himself with chocolate biscuits as well. They were poop-brown and spread all over his moon-round face, and with his cheeks bulging, he never stopped bombarding the newcomers with questions. He wanted to know everything about the dare and its outcome. Max and Finn smiled sheepishly and recounted how they had defeated each of the grudges and freed Jury from the clutches of a bad-tempered security guard.

The ceremony and a few more rules

"What am I hearing? Gaming is a waste of time?!", it rang out. After a short absence Julius had returned to the social hub and had put on a new, virtual outfit.
He was now wearing a full suite of silver armor, with broad shoulder pads that shone and sparkled exaggeratedly. Small, detailed engravings on them told of a heroic battle. A long red cape swung over his back, allowing him to stride majestically through the room.
"Just let the people talk," he said. "Everything you need is here. Here you can do what you want, and you are really free." Julius sounded like a king, proudly presenting his magnificent kingdom. Jury smiled and then they could finally begin: The ceremony.

The Forresters had many rituals. The boys had already been prepared for this on the way to their headquarter and it apparently played an important role not only in joining the team. Whether it was at the end of a successful fight, the drop of a rare item or reaching a new level. All such things were celebrated appropriately and so they should also prepare themselves for a small initiation ritual that was now beginning that evening.

The door with tendrils of maple leaves opened on one side. It led our newcomers into another room. It didn't take much imagination to see something like a throne. Here, too columns formed an open ring. Only this time they were small and angular, and reached so far into an artificial sky that there was no end to it, and thus no roof vault. Only a few flags hung far down and waved in an imperceptible wind.
Between the pillars, impressive pictures could be seen in frames. Powerful creatures were depicted there. They had to be the defeated final bosses, because if you looked at them for a while, their image started to move and in a silent clip, the finish move

with which they were finally defeated was shown.
In the middle was a round platform. It could be reached via small steps made of colored stone. Not marble, but a completely different and bizarre material that emitted light exactly when you stepped on it. Jury's gaze followed glowing footprints that had climbed few steps and led to a high seat. Julius sat down majestically there and looked out at the assembled members.

By now everyone had put on their GG and joined the small group of Forresters, who were pressed closely behind Jury, Max and Finn. Julius first gave an exuberant speech about courage, honor, and the alleged waste of time that they had previously reported from the non-gamers. Then Jury was to step forward and present the key to the eagerly waiting crowd. But first, as tradition dictates, he was to kneel before the admin. An expectant silence spread, until he obediently lowered his head, and his knee touched the ground. Then he opened the inventory and carefully reached out his hand. With a simple "plop", the golden pyramid fell into his hand. An astonished "ooh" and "aah" could be heard.
"You have to shake it," said Julius, and when the respectful voices had died down, Jury shook and rattled the small pyramid until it made a bell-like sound and then finally released its innermost parts. A golden key floated out. It flew a few more inches until it stopped right in front of Jury's eyes. Julius got down from his throne and reached for the key.
"The Forresters have a new level," he shouted and raised the little thing high in the air. Everyone cheered and applauded. Shortly afterwards, Max and Finn also had to step forward and kneel. Now it was time to repeat the rules. According to Julius, they bonded the clan together. But these were not strict laws, he said. Because such things only existed for adults and idiots. Rather, it was a collection of sayings that were supposed to give you a direction when you didn't know what to do next. These rules, which everyone in the clan had to know by heart and in their sleep, were as follows:

1. **Forresters stick together.**
2. **Everyone screws up sometimes, but you never give up.**
3. **All decisions for your team.**
4. **To each his loot.**
5. **Don't talk, do it!**
6. **We make the world as we like it.**
7. **If you are hungry, eat something.**

The order was not based on importance or anything like that, because if someone brought a good or appropriate saying into play, it was simply added to the list. With each new sentence that our three newcomers obediently said, the rest repeated it out loud.

Then it was their turn to choose a fighter class. In Infinity, there was not just one type of player, but the skills and attributes that distinguished them in the game were divided into different classes. For example, there were scouters, sprinters, tanks, magicians and a few more, but the three of them didn't have to think long. They decided on the class they were used to because they knew what they were doing. So, Jury chose the Sprinter. The fast and agile one, whose weapons and armor were designed for quick counterattacks. Max and Finn chose the Scouter as usual. It was a mixture of Sprinter and Tank, similar to Jury's, just a little less speed. But with better defensive capabilities.

After choosing the class, Julius pulled out a purple shimmering short sword. He was also a Sprinter, but he had a slight variation. In the higher levels, he could also fight with swords and other stab weapons. Jury suspected that it must have come from a special event and was visibly fascinated by its simplicity. Because all you needed for it was a simple staff. Nothing more. It didn't even have to be particularly long, because the blade was purely virtual, and the purple glow gave the sword that certain

something. In addition to that it had very special abilities and if you let it rest on your buddies' shoulders long enough, they would automatically be added to the bearer's clan.
And so it was that our three boys were finally accepted, like a knighthood, with all the rights and responsibilities that come with it. A dark electronic voice from Infinity announced this shortly afterwards:
"Welcome to the Forrester clan," it was said, and everyone applauded and cheered loudly and shook the newcomers with countless handholds on their backs. Then came the less pleasant part of the ceremony. Each member had to shake the hand of the newcomer. That's all well and good, you might think, but unfortunately it was also traditional to spit vigorously into your hand before holding it out. One by one they came forward, spitting on each other's hands and congratulating each other, and on top of that, you weren't allowed to wipe it off in between. Some even claimed to leave it dry until the first victory. But you didn't really want to believe it and left it at that.
Last up was Tony's turn. With a cheeky grin, he prepared to shake the newcomers' hands. But this time it took a while. Little Tony pulled out everything that was deep in his throat and then let it slide into his hand in a noisy, slimy, and disgusting manner. There were also a few brown biscuits remains.
"If I didn't know better, you might think this was the real daring," Max said, looking at his hand in disgust and a loud laugh went through the Forresters.

By the fire

Evening arrived quickly. Jury, Max, and Finn were filling their bellies for the first time in what felt like forever. To wash it down, they had lemon soda and a few cookies from little Tony's private stash. Visibly exhausted and with full stomachs, they exchanged a few snatches of conversation, scattered around the social hub's fire on the benches. In the glow of the flames, with his mouth full, Max asked:
"Where do you get all this stuff?"
"Traded for XPs," came a shout from one corner. His name was Chris. At least, that's what everyone called him, and his appearance was no less striking than the others. However, he was the only one who wore a nose ring, and his hair resembled a teased cockscomb. Thick tufts of brightly colored hair were combed back in several strands. This hairstyle was so unusual that it was undoubtedly a virtual one.
Chris explained that you could actually exchange Infinity XP for food vouchers in the G-Stores. That was convenient. That way, you just had to be good at the game, and you wouldn't have to worry about being hungry afterward. This was completely new information for the guys, too, and as the flames of the fire dwindled, the Forresters answered a few of their questions.

Julius explained how the GG worked, and even others were now listening attentively. It was important to have at least some basic knowledge, he said, pointing to the scanner located in the center of the glasses. Every room and environment were measured and transferred to a 3D program running in the background. This allowed any surface or shape to be replaced with a virtual one. Therefore, the scanner, which appeared like a round porthole between the glasses, had to be kept clean and not obscured by any dirt.

"That only leads to mistakes," he emphasized. Each level and all the creatures within it thus adapted to their respective environment. This is why the Groll was able to evade people in the mall. Julius used words like "*dynamic programming*" and Jury, in particular, wanted to know everything in detail. He said nothing, but unlike the others, he stared at Julius demandingly and curiously, so he continued talking despite the increasingly late evening.

The level programming therefore primarily included key data such as position, the player's strength, the number of monsters, and the necessary environmental information, such as the appearance of a cave or building. Even if you entered a different room, the level would adapt based on this information. The calculation was complicated and therefore couldn't be handled by the glasses themselves. They were far too small and compact to perform such complex calculations. It was called *cloud-based computing*. All you needed was a) a high-performance server, preferably with a quantum CPU, and b) a connection with a fast and stable multi-network connection. The GG only delivered the scanner data and received the fully calculated image signals from the connected servers. Depending on the connection and its performance, this happened faster or slower. Nevertheless, you could play every Infinity level anywhere and in any imaginable environment around the world. That was what made it special. Unfortunately, Infinity didn't work at night. The Forresters explained that the gaming servers were shut down on time to prevent nighttime gaming. Too often, the infamous accidents happened this way. Accidents that, logically, weren't good for the developer's business. Sudden collisions, falls from great heights, and so on. Therefore, the night was used for regeneration and battery recharging. But sometimes, as in the case of the dare, there were separate stages. Stages that didn't quite adhere to the basic structure of Infinity. Julius said that the dare involved

chasing the last grudge outside of his territory, all the way to the mall.
"He always did that stupidly at this point," he laughed and continued talking. As a Realgamer you often have to deal with situations that require a certain amount of dedication, without caring what others might think of you.
Jury was increasingly enjoying Julius's explanations. The idea of being different, to insult someone with his actions, and of venturing into a completely new technology, fueled his desire to become a celebrated Realgamer. Jury still had many questions that kept him busy that evening. But when someone yawning loudly, some of them started to leave HQ. It was getting late, and for most of them, it was time to leave. Someone said that otherwise their parents would just worry ridiculously. Jury, Max, and Finn were also asked where they lived and whether their parents are struggling as well with them spending all their free time gaming. The boys hesitated until the questions became more direct, and finally admitted that their parents didn't care. Surprised by this statement, they sat back down again and wanted to know more.
The boys said their parents didn't care what they do all the time, and also that they hadn't been to school for a long term. Some agreed that it was often annoying and was eating up more and more of their free time, and each of them had already missed quite a few lessons. Julius also admitted to skipping some classes to indulge his Infinity addiction. But none of them seemed to be able to imagine a life without parents who resented their everyday lives. For this reason, they first looked skeptical, then surprised and amazed at so much responsibility. Suddenly, the boys were getting the attention they had been waiting for at first. But they didn't want to answer overly direct questions about their families, so the Forresters had to content themselves with their accounts of how they spent their excessive time up to this day.

They talked about their many nights spent gaming as Stationgamers and how, unlike a house or apartment, they were only sleeping on the old upper floor of a dilapidated stairwell. And before they could figure out when to head back there, Julius offered them the opportunity to stay. It wouldn't be a problem at all, because they also stayed here from time to time.
"When things get stressful at home again," he said sympathetically, looking around teasingly and inspiring laughter in the others. But even on vacation or at the weekend, the Forresters made sure to spend most of their time here at headquarters with their friends. Julius brought out a few wool blankets and another added some more wood so that the fire provided pleasant warmth again. Satisfied, the boys agreed. Then everyone set off. Julius also ended the conversation with a curt goodbye. He had class again tomorrow, he said, and from then on, without further explanation, dismissed them into the night.

They had made themselves comfortable around the fire with a few blankets and pillows. The social hub was now bathed in golden light, and it was far too late to start the long walk back to their quarters. The three of them agreed on that. Despite their habit of staying up all night, they had become surprisingly tired that evening. It was probably the eventful day, the full stomach, and the warmth by the fire that had made their limbs feel heavy. With the exception of Jury, they had placed their GGs in a specially designated corner to charge. Conveniently, there was a power bank. One that recharged itself using solar energy. Shortly afterward, Max and Finn fell asleep. Only Jury was still awake, staring up at the ceiling in amazement. Because here, too, the Forresters had let their creativity run wild. Above him, at the top of the dome-shaped room, a real sky stretched out, with beautiful clouds slowly drifting by. And only now did he notice that, with the fall of night, even a few stars were appearing. Simply brilliant, Jury grinned. Because it gave you the feeling of sleeping under the open sky. For a long time, Jury stared at the magical ceiling. Lost in thought, he wondered what his parents were doing at that moment. Were they incredibly sad that he was no longer lying in his bed beneath his self-made solar system as usual, but had simply disappeared? And admittedly, for a brief moment, Jury felt terribly homesick. But fortunately, he wasn't alone. His friends were huddled next to him. And one thing was certain: if he hadn't met them, he would have returned home long ago. But would that have changed anything? Jury didn't believe it and decided to hold out a little longer and wait to see how things developed. An early return would probably have just meant a lot more trouble, which he also dreaded.

The subject of parents was generally unpopular among the three friends. They rarely discussed the matter. Too many things had happened to be able to just get them all out of the way. Talking about it doesn't make it any better, Max once said, and in the dim light of the hallway lamp on their upstairs floor, he hid a worn postcard in his trouser pocket. He had received it from his mother, who now seemed to be living on an island paradise. He carried it with him all the time and guarded it like a treasure. " *With love, your mom,*" was written above a coconut palm tree. Jury and Finn couldn't make out any more and decided not to say another word about parents and family.

Jury also made a move to put his glasses in the corner to charge. But since the battery wasn't dead yet, and he was too tired to get up, he kept them on. The sparkling starry sky had something calming about it, and the Forrester quarters were already crammed with so many fantastical things that there was really no point in taking them off, even for a moment.

The Territory

The Forresters lived on the outskirts of town. It was a long-forgotten area where they had spread, and it must have been at least a decade since factories, warehouses, and companies still conducted their daily business in this place. Between standing walls, cracked windows, empty offices and deserted corridors, you could still find traces left behind by the people who once spent their main part of lives here. Worn shoes, lampshades, squashed food pots, towels, cleaning buckets and faded pictures that told of idyllic flower meadows under a blue sky had been left lying around unnoticed and left to the merciless weather. Weather conditions that reigned supreme in every corner of this almost unreal environment, from spring to winter. But despite all this, the Forrester called this spacious place of disused factory halls, impassable roads, behind the walls overgrown with nettles, their home.

Jury stepped noisily on a cracked bathroom mirror, causing his image to split in two right where he was wearing the GG. Ox, who had gone ahead with Max and Finn, led them through a bare office building and answered some of their questions with a hint of protest. The Forrester used these rooms and their surroundings for their gaming. This was the only way to have enough space to keep the game as fair and simple as possible. According to Ox, in the higher stages it was almost impossible to deal with an overwhelming number of opponents in a confined space. Even innocent people could cause problems. That's why they moved here. Far away from the annoying people of the city and the hustle and bustle of their oh-so-important everyday lives. The Clan didn't get the name from anywhere. It came from the street name where they played and hang out. It was a long, drawn-out worker street, with a few more or less winding outcrops. Named after the successful industrialist *Walter K.*

Forrester, who claimed this part of the city for himself and his own purposes a few decades ago.
The street was dotted with small maintenance and storage buildings between wild and thorn bushes. Now and then, behind elderberry and unidentifiable wild herbs, a few distribution boxes and transformer stations that had been dismantled a long time ago peeked out. And exactly where you might expect to find a few cables, unusable factory material or something similar, Chris lived.

A Sign which says:

- Caution -
High Voltage

was still attached there, and Ox called out his name loudly. Chris had taken off his virtual hairstyle this time, so that he just looked like a regular guy when he opened the door. Pale and with spots on his face, he rubbed his eyes wearily and introduced himself as the team's tactician. Proudly he showed the newcomers his private domain. As a successful tactician, you could probably claim the right to have your own transformer house with a sofa and a freezer. There was no electricity, so that the signs of warning to high voltage inside seemed ironic. A small, high window provided just enough light to avoid bumping into something. Chris had filled this rather small room with all sorts of junk. From personal items such as necklaces made from rusty screws, sunglasses stuck in the holes of a hanging belt, an ashtray made from road tar, to bicycle parts and grease-smeared gears. They probably came from the one he had left next to the transformer box. Then there were shabby magazines with smiling celebrities, trading cards and an oversized movie poster. His current favorite series: The new season of *One Punch Man*, plus an old laptop with a cracked display and a missing enter key. And all of this on a self-made wooden board. Although Chris didn't actually live here but seemed to spend a lot of time at this place.

Because, judging by the freshly crumpled blanket, he also used the tiny sofa corner to get some rest. Chris leaned back there and briefly explained the duties of a tactician.

As such, you had to know about all the stages and levels. But it wasn't enough to just internalize their layout and structure, no, said Chris in a sleepy voice, you also had to know exactly when and where a boss and his adds would enter. In addition, you had to know the respective strengths, weak points, the choice of weapons, armor and then a strong imagination of how an Infinity level would fit together to the gamer's advantage in different and real environments. But that required a lot of experience, he said, and would go too far at this early day - Chris yawned loudly. One pm was simply too early to explain the details of what he was doing, lulled under a thick blanket. And so, several things remained unclear when Ox urged the three boys to move on.

Chris said, he grew up with a lot of social media and all the famous people and celebrities had basically raised him. So, he knew pretty much of them and all famous series and movies for sure as well. Not only the good ones, of course. Because he also likes the real trash. That's why some people called him WEOMPH, said Ox. What *walking encyclopedia of motion picture history* meant. You had to have a good memory for that. You had to be a real brain, as he put it.
For a tactician, Chris seemed pretty unsuited, but Ox assured them that once he had his moments of alertness, he was more than just good. And to conclude with Max's words for that moment: Chris seemed to be ok.

Pimkin

Ox had been given the task by the admin to integrate the newcomers into the clan as quickly as possible. This included an obligatory tour of the premises. Therefore, they were now approaching their next stop.

There was *Pimkin*, for example. A boy not much older than Max or Finn, but in compare to them with a huge big body. Cursing, he kept swinging a metal tube in the heat, which crashed loudly against glass and metal. He was busy beating up a junk car and a description like "chubby" or "fat" simply wouldn't have done him justice, because this boy had probably eaten more than just an extra portion of his daily lunch for years ago. A massive gold chain flashed from broad shoulders that led to a sturdy neck. Unfortunately, it didn't manage to distract from his face. Because there were a lot of pimples sprouting there, which ran from his temples across his bright red cheeks and reached down to a noticeable thick lower lip. So, Max let himself be carried away by one of his usual teasing remarks and hissed something like:
"Wow, what a handsome guy." Jury and Finn suppressed a laugh and asked why he was smashing up that car. Pimkin twisted his mouth and replied:
“Bored. So what?” Then he gritted his teeth angrily and grumbled:
“Rear...wheel...breaker,” as he continued to beat on the car.
“Excuse me?”, asked Max uncharacteristically politely and raised his eyebrows.
"My weapon is called: back...wheel...breaker!" he repeated loudly and did so in such a way that no one knew what he meant and certainly not what to do with this kind of information.
"Well well copied...", Max replied in the same sing-song voice, trying to keep the conversation going. But this huge guy didn't even get it. Tensely, he hit the junk car a few more thundering

blows and then stared into the distance, silent as a soldier on guard duty. He only spoke to Ox. Pimkin obviously had an important matter. It was about some rule that Julius should agree and add to their list, but Ox shook his head and left him standing there without comment.

The boys looked around with interest. Ox explained that Pimkin was always a bit difficult with new members and that they should not worry about his awkward silence. Clearly, Pimkin was not a man of words and Ox explained that he mainly took care of the food supply. It was a job that required the appropriate qualifications, but also responsibility. He was guarding their supplies, somewhat hidden in a garage that could be reached via a parking lot with rusting own less cars. Boxes filled with all kinds of ready meals. Mainly instant soups, pasta, or shrink-wrapped cookies peeked out behind his back through already torn-open packaging. All in all, it was the right task for someone like him. But what kind of job did he have at Infinity? As soon as Jury asked the question, he answered it himself. Pimkin had to be a tank. This fighting class were known by their strength and armor. Everything was designed for defense. No matter how strong a weapon was, a tank needed a lot of damage to even get it into trouble. The only disadvantage: Their health could only recover slowly and with one or two tricks, they could be quickly put out of action. Nevertheless, a tank like him was certainly worth every second.

After the short side seeing tour through the garage and before the boys set off again, Max made one last attempt to start a conversation with Pimkin. Max was actually very experienced in making new friends, but with him he literally bit his teeth on something. After he had even approached him with a friendly smile, he grabbed him by the collar and shouted:
"You are one of Mrs. Eggersfeld's spies! Don´t you?"

“W..what, who??” Max stuttered, while Pimkin pulled Max close to him with puffed-out cheeks:
"Admit it," he hissed. Ox intervened forcefully and freed Max from the sudden embrace.
“Calm down,” he said to Pimkin and began to explain again. Mrs. Eggersfeld was nothing more than a substitute teacher. "With a specialization in unique education," Ox mimicked her in a sharp voice. She attached particular importance to this addition, and it was printed in bold font on one of her numerous business cards. She always held it under the nose of every desperate parent, wherever she went. Despite this, or perhaps precisely because of this, she had declared war on all gamers and gamblers in the world and made it her personal mission to get Pimkin back to math class.
"This woman is a really terrible person," commented Ox, shaking his head and continuing to talk. "A few days ago, she was actually sneaking around our area and since then, he's been... well" - Ox held a hand to his mouth - "quite nervous." Max nodded in understanding and immediately offered him a high five.
"Well then, ...let's work together," he said. But from Pimkin's lips only another grumble and threatening words emerged:
"I know, I have a large frontal lobe," he thundered, "so stop stare at me like a damn animal in the fu*kin` zoo." Max raised his eyebrows again. He hadn't expected to have such conversation partner. But in such cases, he just wasn`t the type of a quitter. Max turned his extended high five into a ghetto fist, smiled, and waited for a reaction again. The whole thing went on until Ox broke the embarrassing situation with a hasty:
“We have to move on,” and everyone set off again.

Shortly afterwards, Finn wanted to know which Forrester rule was mentioned at the beginning. Ox said that Pimkin would like to see one of his rules finally included in the Forrester list, but up until now, there had never been enough for that. His suggestion:

There's no point in complaining, the only thing that really helps is to punch someone in the face very hard. Max and Finn found this kind of wisdom helpful but admitted that it was not important and certainly not among the top ten.
Ox also talked about Pimkin's Realgamer skills and that he was afraid of almost nothing. He had been part of the clan since the beginning and Jury was right in assuming that he was a tank. You had to be brave and tough to be able to face the danger at any time. So, Pimkin was basically afraid of nothing...except for a teacher named Mrs. Eggersfeld.

Flow

Behind an old decayed chemical factory, there was a corrugated iron hut. It protruded from a meadow of wild grass, with knee-high thistles growing in the middle. It was obviously hand-built from countless scrap and individual parts from the area. Some windy breezes seemed to have shaken it, which is why the hut was supported by a wall behind it to give the whole thing more stability. Nails, screws, glue, and bindings were going on here, the boys noticed as they approached it. Between wildly combined boards, colorful plastic sheets and torn-up pressed cardboard, a narrow entrance door could be seen. Countless scribbles could be found there. From comically funny sayings to all kinds of perverted depictions of sexual characteristics. This door must have belonged to a public toilet in its previous life and before anyone could even touch the bent handle, it burst open in a wide arc.
"Don't say a word!" said a disheveled boy and made a theatrical gesture in the air after jumping right in front of his spontaneous visitors. "Because...I can read your future." Our newcomers jumped back in surprise. - So that was *Flow*. - The boy whom Ox had initially described with an embarrassed expression:
"Guys I admit, he's some real weirdo."

Flow had noticeably frizzy hair. Despite the heat, he hid his thick curls under a dirty woolen hat. He only let a few strands dangle over his forehead and face, at the end of which he had woven small colorful stones and neon-colored plastic. Due to his dark skin color, this head of hair stood out somewhat strangely from the rest of his appearance. His skin was so dark that noticeably light edges had already formed where he wore his glasses. This was obviously a stupid side effect of constantly wearing ar-glasses on summer days and probably also the reason why Ox darkened his eyes with makeup as well. No one should be able to

tell at first glance that you were wasting your time with such stupid thing as realgaming, Jury concluded in the back of his mind, and like his friends, he couldn't quite understand how he had overdone it with the make-up. Not only were his eyes hidden under a thick, black-blue layer of paint. He had also drawn long white lines on his cheeks and forehead, so that he almost looked like a native American just in black. Feathers were also tied to his hat and hair, which he had obviously found here on the grounds and eagerly collected.
Flow invited his visitors in, overexcited but friendly. He pointed to a kind of seating circle in the middle of the rather dark dwelling. The boys entered and looked around curiously. Flow in meanwhile, was rummaging excitedly in one of the many corners that he obviously used as storage space. Looking for something. He kept babbling some incomprehensible scraps of speech and threw the things he pulled out, which obviously did not correspond to his idea, loudly across the misshapen Space.
"Ah, there it is," he was heard. Flow pulled out an old, dirty parka and immediately threw it over himself with a flourish. It was much too big and wide for his slender stature, so that it was more like a long cape with a big hood. Or like a colorful patchwork quilt. Every hole that had been torn in it had been hastily patched up with all sorts of scraps of fabric and everything else in the room looked exactly like Flow's cape. You had the feeling of being inside an oversized pile of found objects that had been hollowed out in the middle.
In one corner lay a broken mirror with an ornate frame. Glued and only partially repaired. Right next to it, knives, and blades without handles, hanging from a slight turning bicycle tire with bent spokes. Then shoes, sneakers, boots in all sorts of different variations and colors. In between them, an egg holder from a freezer, with homemade figures made of silver foil stuck in it. Colorful shoelaces, dolls' heads and other things hung from above, where a bright cone of light strayed here and there. Thick flakes of dust rose in them, causing Max to sneeze loudly. He

needed a moment to catch his breath and soon discovered a wooden bowl in the middle of the circle of seats.
"Oh, great some cracker," he said and grabbed them boldly, but Max pulled a face. "Wow... that kind takes some getting used to," he joked, but still choked it down greedily. "I would call the taste; *Soogou.* Some shit out of grandma's old underwear."
Suddenly Flow rushed over and snatched the bowl out of his hands in horror.
"Are you fu*kin nuts?!" he raged, pausing for a moment before continuing with a meaningful expression in dramatic hand gesture: "This is...my damn SEER bowl," said Flow in a serious way, but shortly afterwards he put on an overly friendly face again. Well, he couldn't be mad at the newcomers. They didn't know any better, he said. The boys exchanged communicative glances while Flow sorted the potato crackers back in position, into a certain order. But despite their ignorance, he apparently had reasons to be mad. After all, none of them had been waited for him to be there for the inauguration ceremony.
"I think that was really mean of you," he snapped at Ox, "You knew I had important things to do in town. You just had to wait a bit." Ox rolled his eyes and replied to Flow's angry words with nothing but a smile. Flow, on the other hand, kept talking and explained that he now had to perform another, very important ritual. Time was apparently short. None of a Forrester should become Realgamer without appropriate spiritual support. That would be a very bad karma, he said, and the boys should please sit down immediately.
Jury and Max crouched on an upturned metal bucket. Finn and Ox sat down instead on two converted drinks crates, where old trousers and unidentifiable items of clothing were tied together to form a cushion. Flow handed them a kind of tea in strangely converted cups. These had clearly once been the headlights of a car. Jury, Max, and Finn exchanged incredulous glances, which shortly afterwards wandered questioningly to Ox. But he just rolled his eyes again, calmly sipped this hopefully stomach-

friendly brew and hid a sudden fit of laughter behind his cup. Flow in meanwhile, set about what he called his "job" and between a multitude of small boxes with illegible labels and a considerable collection of all kinds of shoes, he dug out something like a rattle. Dented corrugated cans with loudly clinking contents were tied to a stick, which he now spun in a crazy dance in front of the boys' eyes. From time to time, he stammered spontaneously made-up fantasy words like: "Komundal Saladar" or "Hie Watou, Watou Asalada." Then he went back into a rhythmic dance again and after what felt like endless embarrassing minutes, as if somebody let one fly and no one wants to bring it up, he leaned over the bowl of cracker chips what seemed like a trance and whispered:
"The oracle sees." Then he put his hand to his forehead, accompanied by an exaggerated cry of pain. "The oracle sees..." he whimpered, his eyes wide open, and an equally long-term moment of awkward silence followed. And when Max was already stirring impatiently in his seat, Flow said in a flash:
"I see - dramatic pause - I see... turbulent times coming your way, with ups and downs."
Flow filled the room with another pain-filled scream, before sinking exhausted into a large pillow. The boys looked at each other in questions. Flow didn't move at all until Max asked disparagingly:
"Are we done?"
Flow sat up awkward and confused, he took a bottle of soda from one of the corners, took a big swig and stammered:
"I don't know if I still have the strength to spit in your hands, as tradition dictates."
"Oh, that's fine," Finn answered on behalf of everyone. "Uh, yeah, exactly," did the others agree. With the last dancing and stammering of *Asalada thing*," they had already gotten enough of his spit, mentioned Max.
Flow nodded gratefully and tried to pull himself together and when everybody thought this situation of embarrassing himself

was over, he screams to the boys right away with his eyes wide open:
"But there is one more thing!" Max and Finn groaned and sat down again. "You guys have to know it", he said out of breath, in a serious manner. "I noticed... someone of you has a deep... HIDDEN secret."
"Ja okay, we got it", said Max annoyed.
"But I felt..., oh gosh, I cannot say it", he whimpered. "I felt it is a dark one" and looked around wildly with some wtf-expression. "And when your story with the Forrester goes on, it will be uncovered."
"That`s nice to hear", Finn argued friendly and tried to get up.
"But obviously you don't understand", pushed Flow him back into the seat. "A complete cure cannot be promised", he said. "Friendship brings healing but cannot save everyone." Then Flow acted like he had to calmed down again and from then on talked as if nothing had happened, as if he had just woken up from a bad dream. Told them insistently what unique role he played in the Forrester clan, especially with Infinity.

Flow was a so-called *seer*. In the game, seers had the ability to use magic. It meant some kind of Magician, Healer, and Wizard all packed in one. So, you didn't need to fight with the usual firearms, but with different hand movements that performed a wide variety of actions depending on how they were used. While Ox used the dry term *"gesture control"*, Flow spoke dramatically about lightning storms, pressure waves, protective force fields and even level-changing abilities. But you didn't have to fully understand them. The only important thing to know was that every clan needed such so-called "spiritual leader" who would not only guide you safely through the dangerous stages of Infinity, but also took care of the members' little aches and concerns. He had healing powers, he emphasized, and was firmly convinced that he could simply sweep away any horrible illness. Whether it was a pimple, a rash, or stomachache, it was no issue at all. You just had to register in good time, because a capable seer like him is always busy. In that case was it a bit strange that after the boys had finished their tea and were about to leave, Flow begged them to stay. The boys hesitated, but finally sat down again.

Flow obviously didn't quite understand the difference between gaming and realness. In all seriousness, he talked about countless spontaneous healings that he had already performed and proofed, and the guys weren't sure whether he was talking about Infinity or the real life. In any case, he proudly presented his equipment shortly afterwards, followed by a detailed presentation of various seer outfits. There was also a fashion show of coolly designed arm and leg protectors, plus visually coordinated magician capes and very much more. Everything that a seer would need in his opinion. Without being asked, Flow talked about his various specials and features, where to find them and which perks, he was still missing. And of course, how often he had already used them successfully and which trophies and stages he had already earned for the clan. In conclusion, he put itself out to be some kind of game changer.
All well and good, surely interesting, but that didn't say anything about himself. About his past, his backstory. Why and how he came to be a Forrester. Why they called him *Flow*. How long he had been here and so on. Every conversation began and ended in some way with and about the game. Infinity was the only thing in every small talk and Jury's guess was simple. Before his life as a gamer, Flow was apparently a Crab. You didn't have to be a genius to recognize that. Because he had obviously never been able to shake off the strong passion for collecting and hunting trash that was reflected in every corner of his hut. Something the crabs were born with. But in compared to others, Flow's life was in no way poorer or less comfortable. Only the mighty holes in his hut suggested that it could get uncomfortable here when the weather get changed. But when they asked why he didn't sleep in

one of the surrounded buildings or even in the social hub, Flow just smiled and explained proudly that he had built this hut with his own hands.
"Anyone who knows the feeling, who knows what it's like to create something by yourself, would never want to miss it again," he said with proud and offered the boys another batch of his questionable concoction. But this time they had to decline with thanks, because Ox, as always, urged them to move on. Shortly afterwards, the toilet door of Flow's hut slammed shut, so that Max immediately complained:
"Turbulent times are coming. Pah! I could have read something like that from a bowl of moldy potato chips as well." Max questionably rubbed his stomach and Ox laughed out loud for the first time.
Jury noticed Max apparently tried to cover up something in that situation. Maybe he was the one with the dark secret. But for Jury that couldn`t be, and in one thing maybe Flow was right: Obstacles had to overcome.

That afternoon, the boys checked out several locations. Although they walked up and down Forrester Street several times and they still didn't feel like they had seen everything. Too winding and too interwoven was this place, so big that it probably would take days to see everything at least once and to save it all in memory. From start to finish, they had visited everyone who lived outside of the headquarter in between rotten Buildings grounded at lost places. There were some who welcomed the boys in a friendly manner, while others eyed them suspiciously from a safe distance. They probably perceive the newcomers as competitors and only changed a few words if necessary. Everyone in the clan obviously had fixed tasks, which someone else could have taken over if they failed. For this reason, Jury in particular could understand their skepticism because where they would fit in remained had to be seen.

Land of the Unbending

Strange plants grew on a lonely meadow. Ornamental palms and cacti, which towered over the grass like imaginative watchtowers, had managed to establish themselves here. Winter was evidently not hard enough to drive them away. Otherwise, there was nothing earth-shattering far and wide. At the end of their side seeing tour, Ox took the boys to a lonely spot of wild undergrowth and extensive footpaths. Paths behind a slope of dense trees, blocked the view of the distant Forrester Road. Nothing else was there to discover. The only thing that was conspicuous was a pile of rubble that protruded like a rock from the colorful sea of grass. Shrugging their shoulders, the three looked around and wondered why he had brought them to such place.

"This is the land of the Unbending", he said pompous and explained that each of them was assigned their own space on the grounds, which they could use for their own purposes and interests, so to speak. A kind of *Relax-Place* (RP), where you had the opportunity to retreat. Aside from its cool name, the good spots were apparently already given to the higher members of the clan, Max hissed, so that unfortunately only this patch of fallow meadow remained. You can let off steam here, said Ox. Get imagination run wild. Infinity supposedly offered unimagined possibilities to really spice up such an inconspicuous place.

"Make the world as you like," he stiffly recited one of Forrerster's rules, trying to put a positive spin on the whole thing. But his feigned euphoria didn't rub off the boys. Visibly disappointed, they let their gaze wander over the meadow and the pile of rubble that was probably infested with countless spiders.

"Can't we find another place?" asked Max.

"Exactly, we'll find something better," Finn agreed and immediately continued walking. He followed the path over the

slope, where at the end, thickly grown trees covered an adjacent wall.
"Not that way," Ox shouted annoyed. But it was too late. Curious they sprinted after him, only to soon come across an iron door in the middle of the overgrown wall made of crumbling bricks.
"We're not allowed to go there," Ox shouted in a serious tone. But Finn and Max were already shaking the rusty handle, until the door gave way.

Everything was dark inside. Light only came in through broken windows on the upper floor. Your eyes had to get used to it before you could gradually see anything. It was a large room made of cold concrete, but otherwise completely empty. Countless graffiti you could find on the walls. Strange characters and symbols, mixed with all kinds of colors and numbers. Nearly, there wasn't a single empty spot to be found and even the ceiling, which was hard to reach, was not spared. There were thick traces of paint on the floor too. Strange. Someone seemed to have let his creativity run wild here or some crazy dude under drug abuse got caught like a rat in a trap and was just bored.
"Well... quite possible," Max commented, suspecting the work of a madman. An escaped psycho who probably suffered from something like "post-traumatic anxiety disorder."
“Don’t you think maybe he was just bored,” Finn suggested Max.
"Then it must have been a very terrible boredom," he replied and prepared to explore the rest. Jury had already approached the end of the room and a crumbling landing that led to the next floor when Ox stood angrily into the door.
"Stop," he shouted. "Are you crazy?! This is forbidden territory!"
“Why is it forbidden?” they asked.
“Because this is the border!”
“A border of what?”, wanted Max to know immediately.
"The border of the Forrester territory," replied Ox, pointing to an inconspicuous blob of red paint that someone had painted on the iron door. "This sign represents the end of our territory," he said.

"Remember it. You don't know any better. But now you know it and you will stick to it. Otherwise, that's it for your adventure as Realgamers. Got it? Let's go." Suddenly there was a scream. It was Jury.

“What’s up?” Max shouted and immediately came running with Finn.

"Over there, ... there's something," Jury stammered anxiously and pointed to a dark spot from which something was staring at him. Everyone tried to make out something until suddenly Max said disappointedly:

"You idiot. I thought you'd found a dead bum but it's just a drawing. Look." And indeed, on one of the walls there was a dark graffiti that had terribly frightened Jury. A truly sinister face was visible, which, after upon closer inspection, protruded from a kind of storm front. Lightning shot out of the middle and formed the outline of a horrific figure. White glowing Eyes without pupils stared out of them and the outline of a hooked mouth could be seen. There were also claw-covered paws that were about to grab the viewer and pull him into the scene. Demonic and powerful, clearly not of this world. This picture was so terrifying and at the same time just as beautiful that it could only have been created by the hand of a true artist.

“What is that?” asked Jury in astonishment and his hand hardly daring to touch the wall on which this extraordinary figure was drawn.

"It's a warning," Ox said, pushing the iron door open further so it could be seen better.

“A warning?” asked Max skeptically.

“About what?” Finn replied.

"Don't you recognize it?" said Ox and the boys exchanged questioning glances. "That's damn Sacoon!"

“Sa..coon?”

"You're kidding me," Ox raged. "You really don't know who that is? SACOON, the absolute meanest final boss of all time. The prime evil and final boss of Infinity."

Ox said that this strange thing was creeping through the Infinity levels. It would randomly appear somewhere and then go hunting for gamers. Luckily, he only encountered it once. You had to try to avoid it somehow and if it did spot you, you just had to run. Because you couldn't actually kill it.
"Not yet," he said, pointing his finger. "Oh man. It's going to be a wild party when we finish it. I can barely wait for it.
At the bottom of the wall, he kicked a few empty spray cans aside, so that the work could be viewed in its entirety. Below it was written by hand:
"Just 12 t XPs and you're screwed." Julius had sprayed the Sacoon on this wall as a daily warning for all Forresters. The saying was also from him, and Finn immediately wanted to know what the XPs were all about. The number was obviously no longer up to date, said Ox, but it was the experience points that the clan still needed to take part in the big event. Jury, Max, and Finn looked at each other again and only managed a short murmur:
"Event?" Ox then gave his almost usual wtf-look.
"YES, the event," he repeated demandingly. "The big topic of the whole city? What every gamer has been working towards for the last few months?!" Ox was apparently waiting for one of the boys to ring a bell. But nothing happened. Even Jury was surprised that he had missed this kind of information. Maybe it was because they had only recently become official Realgamers, or because not every piece of information in their district was displayed on an oversized poster. But the fact was: The Clan were looking forward to a very special event.

It was an event especially for Realgamers. Since there existence it took place every year. It was the so-called Final Battle, where only the best of the best gets together. The conditions were simple. You just had to pass all the levels and also reach a certain number of experience points. Only the clans that fulfilled these conditions could take part and thus got the unique chance to defeat Sacoon, the meanest final boss of all time. The reward they quoted was the following sentence:

***Honor and glory forever,
for whom the Sacoon strikes down in a fair and glory fight.***

In addition, unique items and a decent amount of prize money awaited. Ox's eyes lit up as he continued speaking in an unusually cheerful manner:
"Fame forever! Do you understand?! We all will be famous. Everyone will know our name," his words echoed through the empty room. All the clan needed was to complete the levels and reach a certain EP number and they could join in. There were only three left to complete, but Ox did not want to say how many XPs the Forresters needed to take part and hemmed and hawed when asked. All he said was:
"You'll see. We still have a lot of work ahead. But we can do it."
“So, you can only defeat the Sacoon in the final battle?” said Jury, almost disappointed, and Ox nodded.
"And what are these symbols?" asked Finn, who suddenly looked around the room with interest. "They're tags, aren't they?"
"Oh no”, Ox replied. "They don't mean anything. It's just some nonsense. Come on, let´s get out of here." Then he pushed everyone out of the door and when they were out, he took one last look around inside. He seemed nervous for a moment. Then with a single swing, Ox closed the iron door.

At the top of the wall, where the grass was already above their knees, the boys took a break at the place that had been assigned to them to relax. Maybe they could get used to it after all. So, they pondered and discussed. But if you thought it was just a question of where and what to put here, you were wrong. Because a very one question quickly arose: What is actually a place to relax? Because even on this apparently simple point, opinions differed considerably.

One thought a football pitch wouldn't be bad, another a crazy skater park would be a good idea, and the last one actually suggested a huge fairground with colorful lights and rides. "Nonsense!" was only be heard and before it turned into a sensible argument, Ox realized that he had to intervene. In a strong voice, he made it clear that Max would be the best suited for this task. Max, on the other hand, hesitated and pulled his face. But Ox made it a point that day. Max was to be the one who would pimp up this place in a suitable virtual way. Shortly afterwards, Jury and Finn also talked to him. With a pat on the shoulder, they said:
"Oh, you'll think of something good." Because secretly they were glad that this rather stupid task had fallen to him. And while Jury would much rather find out more about this finale battle, Finn tried to pull himself up to a good spot on that wall to explore the rest of the area. But Ox held him back with serious words. Because everyone who lived here had to follow the rules. Ox explained it like this:
"No one enters the other's territory without a valid reason." He did not want to answer who this “other” was and not explain what they were doing here as well. The whole area was thus strictly divided and behind this brick wall, the Forrester's territory just ends. So, there were boundaries for a Forrester too. Ox himself pointed between the bushes to a red symbol that had been sprayed on a rotten cardboard box there. It was supposed to be an intertwined *T* and *O*, which meant something like *taboo.*

Realgamers Life

The Forresters were sitting close together. A small circle had been formed around the fire of the social hub, which bathed their faces in a soothing golden light. Above it, a wildly assembled creation from Pimkin's garage sizzled in a pan. Between the crackling fire and the loud smacking of the hungry, one could also hear some odd laughs. The mood was exuberant. Now that everyone was gathered, mates ate and discussed loudly. The final battle was the big topic. It was getting closer and closer, and not only the higher-ranking members of the clan, like Julius, Ox, or tactician Chris, but everyone else had something to say about it.

The event changed its location every year, moving from city to city, so to speak and you could hardly believe the luck, this time it took place here. But when Julius said “here”, he didn’t mean Forrester Street, but rather the famous stadium in the city center. For such an event, only public buildings were chosen. Chris used the term "hard area". In other words, an setting where the shape and size are fixed. This meant that all the competing teams were treated with absolute equality and fairness. For this reason, each of them was busy trying to find out exactly what XPs could be achieved in the game. The only thing was, the more they talked about it, the more unsure Jury, Max, and Finn became about whether they could meet the requirements. Not only were their armor and weapons still in the early stages, but with regard to their experience and skills, it was still completely unclear whether they could be of any real help to the Forresters. Finn and Max agreed that this would probably take weeks and made their doubts clear with tense looks and head scratches. For this reason, the guys scheduled a *Zone Control session* (SCS) right the next day. A variation of the good old *Capture the Flag* (CTF), which was intended to prepare the three for the seriousness of Realgamers life. Julius himself wanted to hold a brainstorming on the right choice of weapons and armor in the early hours of the morning right before school. This was crucial in order not to end up as "fresh meat" or "PvP victim". At least that was what Chris said, who joined in the conversation later. He pulled a stick with something on it out the fire and philosophized with Julius about the life as a gamer. What status you could achieve with it, how many guys had already sent him a friend request and who was practically begging for membership in the clan. People were always coming up with new ideas to draw attention to themselves. After all, everyone, without exception, wanted to be at top. The gamers with the highest level were literally worshipped, idolized by the community. Not only Chris and Julius liked that, as you could tell from their tone of voice, but also Jury. Besides the fire, he listened to the two of them with interest and when Julius noticed him, he waved him over. Julius asked if he had settled in, and introduced everyone much more personally. This was important in order to avoid stupid mix-ups in confusing fights. Jury nodded with understanding and told how he had also discovered his huge graffiti of the sacoon during the tour. Jury tried to steer the conversation in the desired direction, because he didn`t want to learn about the final boss only through Ox's terse words. He praised the well-made picture and this dark image of the boss had long since eaten its way deep into his thoughts. Jury was consumed by the thought of one day actually standing before him. Julius shared this opinion and provided plenty of fuel for the fire of enthusiasm with embellished details. He reported on a few of his encounters with this sinister creature.

No one could say exactly what it looked like. That was because it was constantly changing its shape, like the clouds in the sky. Some people therefore called it a mystical dual creature. It supposedly came from an unknown dimension and paid a short and cruel visit to ours at regular intervals.

At one point, the Sacoon walked straight towards Julius. Luckily, it hadn't seen him yet, so he was able to hide behind a ledge.

Snorting and greedily, you could hear it searching for him. But if you didn't move and stayed completely still, said Julius, it was difficult for it to locate you. But many people lose all their coolness just by seeing them or being near to them, he said, so they just run away screaming. And if you caught the Sacoons attention, you didn't just lose items and weapons, the whole team had to start all over again. Only on the day of the final battle did you have the chance to face it fairly, he said, and in euphoric words he told everything about the event.

In more than 100 countries, the event was broadcast live on all channels. Someone played a clip to jog your memory. It was simply projected somewhere in the room. This was no big deal with GG either. In any case, the competing teams were driven through an oval arena in crazy monster trucks. It was unmistakably reminiscent of a futuristic alien ship. Crowds cheered. Then confetti rained down, sparkling like little stars, and trickling down in slow motion. Booming, powerful beats, colorful spotlights in the haze. Flashes of light. People screaming wildly, waving, dancing, or greeting into the camera. And then, deep down in the middle of all this hustle and bustle, where everyone's eyes were gathered, they stood. The Realgamers! Each looking proud and awed. The suits of armor and outfits were its own individual work of art. In their faces: anticipation and enthusiasm. And every now and then, when a group called out their name, they looked up to the crowd, where their clan's banners were flying. In animated formations, far above the people. Everyone called out their name. Until the never-ending storm of applause was simply swept away by the long-awaited and deeply trembling start sound of the final battle.

After the clip ended and Julius had discussed each of their moves tactically with others, he was not only grilled by Jury. Finn and Max, who had joined them in the meantime, also asked a lot of questions. Among other things, they were again about the experience points earned, the levels required and even, as Finn said, about the ridiculous taboo sign that he had spotted in other places on the grounds. But Julius argued against his negative attitude, this would not get the clan any further. Being a Forrester also meant loosening up a bit, not seeing everything so doggedly and letting coolness flow into your body from time to time. His words were something like that, which caused some laughter in behind. Julius obviously did not like Finn's general manner. The newcomers should first think of a suitable name for their weapon before their worries consumed them. That would be just as important as the attitude he wanted. Julius soon made it clear to the boys that every gamer would have to create his very own weapon during his career and without any suitable name no one would remember.

So, now you might think that a right and cool naming a weapon would be an easy and quick matter, a fun part so to speak, but that's far from it. The boys quickly realized that the coolest and most sonorous ones were somehow already have been taken. Nevertheless, some of the Forresters didn't stop throwing a new one into the ring at regular intervals. With a snap of his fingers, little Tony was the first to come up with a suggestion:

"*Egg slicer,*" he said. But the newcomers turned up their noses.

"What about *home alone*?" said Chris. Finn nodded until Max shook his head.

"*Dreambreaker,*" came from Ox, but that didn't seem to suit their taste either, whereupon Pimkin intervened:

"Mine already has the best name, but what about: *My answer to math test.*"

"Oh well," Flow interjected and rolled his eyes.

"Do you have anything better?", replied Pimkin angrily.

"Yes, I do," said Flow and immediately checked the newcomers' reaction:

"Widow maker...or maybe...mother's tear maker."

"Hmm... I don't know", said Max, trying to convince the others that they surely needed a little longer to think about it. But suddenly the Forresters didn't seem to care. Instead, a real challenge emerged between Flow and Pimkin as to who had the better suggestion. So, they stood up, faced each other in eager to argue. Then they called out their names like a curse word, and some of the suggestions weren't that bad at all. The others just enjoyed the show and incited the scene with a provocative "Uhh" or "yes, show him".

"Insatiable," shouted the first one.

"Ass spreader," replied the other.

"Twass - That´s what she said," was the quick reply.

"Back Scratcher 6.0"

"Air polluter"

"Gravedigger"

"Surgery Victim"

"Tormentor"

"Bone mill"

"Shut up and die"

"Gender Changer Free"

"Hospice room occupant"

"Brain smoothie"

"Like a second belly button?"

"Intestinal spindle"

"Escalation instead resignation"

"Surgical Intervention 2.0"

"Bacon rind massacre"

"Cringe Lord"

"Elon Musk"

"Blood transfusion regulator"

"Rear wheel spiral staircase machine"

And a lot more followed. But whoever won the challenge was lost in laughter and in confusion of gossip of the others that continued. But in anyway, it didn't matter because sooner or later, the next challenge would be ahead and appoint a new, short-term winner.

Later, due to Julius' skillful evasive maneuvers, Jury wanted to know whether they would also be able to be ready on that special day of the event. Whether they too would have the chance of enjoying this spectacle. Julius grinned.
"First, you should think of a really cool name for your weapon," he said. "Then, we will see", and in a friendly manner he assured him in the light of fire that their future lay before them in bright sparkling letters.

Dreams

Jury jumped up. It was night and the fire in the social hub had already burned down. Only the light from the remaining embers cast shadows over the benches. Max and Finn quickly fell asleep and none of the others were there. Jury sat up and reached out for his GG. Shortly before tiredness overcame him, he had put it down next to him. To be able to see better, he put it on. A simple night vision app made it possible. Flow had kindly downloaded it for him and swore by its usage, because at night, not a single streetlamp shone on the premises.
A strange dream had Jury woken up. It was somehow about a fight, the Sacoon and the name of his weapon. Because he still hadn't thought of a good one. Sleepy and confused, he looked around. But before he could dig back under the warm blanket to perhaps catch up a better and more beautiful dream, he had to relieve himself first in order do some Toilet stuff. He must have drunk too much soda that night as he sat and talked near by the fire. So, he slipped in shirt and shoes, which he found right next to his sleeping place, and left the room with quiet steps.

The headquarter, so called social hub, was inside an old but well-preserved factory hall. There were only a few holes, which the Forresters had patched and repaired, so that the wind and rain couldn`t enter anymore. The wide and long Forrester Street bordered directly on the hall's entrance, which led through a heavy and creaking door. Now there was silence in this place. Only the wind made a few timid noises. Strange noises. And just as strange how the night changes an entire place, thought Jury and took a few steps to approach one of the inviting bushes. When he was finished and just about to make his way back, he noticed a light. At first, he guessed it was just his imagination. But on a second glance he saw some kind of shimmer. It was green and moving noticeably back and forth at the end of the road, where empty houses towered up like black monsters. Curious, Jury awoke from his daze. Apparently, they were not alone on the site after all, as they had been told. Certainly, it would have been smarter to just turn around and go back right away to the SH, but Jury felt compelled to follow it. He just had to be careful and stay inconspicuous, then no one would notice him. So, he walked quietly and approached the mysterious light. But following it was not so easy. Because shortly afterwards, when he reached the end of the street, it was flying and dancing around. For a moment it even disappeared behind a building, only to reappear in another place. Jury also thought he had seen the shadow of a cape moving hastily in the night. Obviously, someone was walking around on their property, he concluded, and he would not let himself be shaken off. He followed the green light until it disappeared behind a door between bushes at the edge of a meadow. Jury also went in there. Perhaps a single look inside would answer his questions, and so, he found himself in the stairwell of a dark and eerie building.

Water dripped from a leaky drainpipe. You couldn't say exactly where it came from, because the dripping echoed through a dark maze of hallways and even drowned out Jurys cautious steps. Despite Flow's app, only the outlines of the walls and doors that led into even darker rooms could be seen. But it was enough to orientate himself and avoid colliding with anything. Shortly thereafter, some light illuminated the way, and you could smell the wet stone of old walls. And whoever Jury had followed must have run deeper into the building or disappeared into one of the many rooms. But he didn't want to go any further. Perhaps at least to the end of the next corridor and when he got there, his feet just kept walking, as if they wanted to at least buy some time before the logical part of mind finally prevailed.
Behind a bend, which split into two new paths, Jury noticed an open door with a faint light shining through it. It took him a moment to recognize the Forrester taboo sign on it. Despite this,

or perhaps because of it, he went on and looked inside apprehensively. In one corner, he saw a strange object almost hidden on the floor. Something like a ball. One that wasn't just lying on the floor but was laying in something like a goblet-like container. Almost in a transparent shape it appeared and changed its color in pulsating bursts like a will-o'-the-wisp. First yellow, then green, which changed to blue, and when you come closer finally became a strong red.
Jury was amazed and could not believe what was lying right at his feet. He carefully crouched down to reach out a finger. But his fingertip only approached slowly, waiting for something unexpected to happen. Suddenly Jury heard a noise. It came from one of the corridors. Then footsteps followed. At the same moment the room darkened. Jury turned back and the strange ball that had just been pulsing in front of him like a glowing heart had disappeared. Only the strange holder was still there, nothing else. Jury did not think twice and quickly went back to where he had come from. This place was too spooky, he thought, and made his way back as quickly as he could. But when he reached the stairwell, voices suddenly rang out.
They were clearly audible, and Jury paused and listened for a moment. To his surprise, they sounded familiar. They echoed from one of the upper floors. Under the cover of darkness Jury moved forward and followed the suspicious sounds, until he reached a large room with only a few stairs up and couldn't believe his eyes.

A dim light illuminated the middle. A fire was burning high under the ceiling. But to be precise, it wasn't a fire. It was a white flame that was stuck in a tube-like funnel made of glass and blazed away inside. Below it, a structure of gnarled branches and snake-like outgrowths was forming in supple lines, which emerged from a stone table underneath.
The table was formed from countless faces, bodies, and squiggles. All of them protruded from a pitch-black, viscous mass.

In some way it even moved and like a water spring, gushed out of the middle of the floor in slow, bubbling spurts. The path to this middle was lined with several statues. They were carved from rough, sharp-edged stone and formed the dark silhouettes of strange creatures in metallic armor. Their large, protruding eyes, set in a cruelly face, were tightly closed and their gaunt arms, with claws instead of hands, clutched an iron spear made of barbs in a hunched posture. On the walls, rows of ancient torches hung on small pedestals. But their light had long since gone out, however, because nothing but darkness filled the rest. And right there, hidden in dark, Jury crouched and stared at the illuminated center, where a large altar could be seen. In front of that were two persons, whom he immediately recognized. They were Ox and Chris. They talked to each other and seemed to be pondering something. Jury remained silent and only rarely let his head peek out from behind one of the statues. The two were discussing a riddle that needed to be solved and were examining a skull that was positioned conspicuously close to the table. It was about a witch who was to be summoned and questioned in order to get another clue. They also talked about the newcomers. Would they really be any help for the clan? Ox sighed skeptically, while Chris was apparently operating a mechanism. Because suddenly the eyes of the statues began to open, and life came into their bodies. A bright yellow light burst from their limbs and the creatures, which had initially been frozen, stood up. Groaning, they turned one after the other to the altar and illuminated a spot there, which triggered another clicking mechanism. Then you could hear a hissing sound in a shallow mist and a small rectangular chamber rose from the black spring. It looked like a cage, which opened immediately. Out came a tiny and bony creature wearing an oversized silk cloak with a hood, as clothing. Ox and Chris had to bend down to look in to the small, bizarre face. After a moment of silence, it began to speak loudly. But it was more like a screaming. The little thing cursed and struggled until it answered some of their questions in a sketchy and whining manner:

"...only the one who carries the zeal of a mighty god can help you..."

That was all Jury understood before the strange witch quickly went back into her cage and, without taking a single breath, sank into the black liquid.
Ox and Chris walked around thoughtfully. They pondered what she could have meant and repeated some of her enigmatic words. Suddenly Chris stopped talking and turned to the statues. He thought he had heard something and pointed a suspicious finger at a dark spot in the room. It was the spot where Jury was crouching. He quickly flinched and hid deep in the shadows. Ox confirmed that he had felt like he was being watched for some time and then walked purposefully forward. He headed straight to the one spot that was now only few steps away from him. Each of them was almost like a countdown that was ticking down inexorably. Jury tried not to breathe. Ox looked into the corner and was frightened. Because suddenly something shot out of it. Squeaking and hopping, it darted across the floor between his feet. It was a rat. While Ox annoyedly gave the all-clear, Jury had rushed unnoticed down the stairs to the exit and when he reached the open meadow again, he ran as fast as he could back to the social hub.

“Hey, wake up!” Jury opened his eyes. He recognized Max in blurry features.
"You were talking in your sleep again" he said as Jury looked at him confused. Max pulled on his shirt. "Must a been a nightmare, he?"
“Yeah...nightmare,” Jury replied, letting her head fall back in relief.

Lock jaw, the zeal of Zeus and a music teacher

"The ARW 224 has the following characteristics," Julius began to explain like a Major General. They had arranged to meet on a dusty square near the social hub. A virtual flag was waving majestically there, bearing the Forrester coat of arms. It showed two F's facing each other, forming a kind of T-shaped military symbol, drawn in gold on a rich green, with a proud eagle with broad wings underneath.

The morning sun had already risen to sweaty heights when Julius spoke to a small group consisting of the newcomers, Flow, Tony and Pimkin and insisted on keeping his announced briefing.
The others were still at home or school at this daytime and as Flow said, were being held by their parents.
Julius introduced the boys to an impressive weapon. It was specially designed for RGs. The company that invented Infinity also came up with released so-called ARWs. This abbreviation stood for *Augmented Reality Weapon*. But even that was probably a too long term for a Realgamer. Therefore, the first two letters were simply left out and the English *"double-u"* was only used as *"doub"* when talking about such weapon.
In any case, there were a wide variety of models and in contrast to the otherwise cobbled together junk that almost every RG used, were these guns, to put it in the words of Max:
"The absolute amazing shit."
Not only did they look stylish, but they also had a dynamic trigger with integrated vibration feedback. Plus, an interchangeable magazine, Buttons for switching back and forth from single to rapid fire and a practical carrying strap. And on top of that: A recoil simulator plus, additional sensors that simulate perfect muzzle flash in the game.
Unfortunately, the Doubs were almost unaffordable for an average twelve-year-old without a summer job or rich parents, so

Julius now had to endure the greedy looks of the others. No one dared to ask where he got them from. His parents were probably showing their love and affection, or rewarding him for his rare, good grades in school. But at least everyone was allowed to try them out and take aim at one or two targets with different firepower. The only one who was critical was Finn. He said that you didn't need much skill to get a kill with a gun like that. But he spoke so quietly that Julius couldn't hear it. Although most of the time he actually fought with a sword. He owned several of these weapons. Some of the clan members were even allowed to use them, but many of them were previous models or a cheap copy of the original presented here. Unfortunately, due to the heavy use, they were already completely broken and worn out. You could admire them in the holders in the armory. But each of was password protected and of course reserved only for die-hard gamers. The three of them weren`t yet among them, but Jury hoped that one day he might be able to call one of these Doubs his very own. In the meantime, the self-made ones would have to suffice, whose abilities were only shown in the virtual world. Overnight, each of the boys had thought of a name, which they now proudly presented to the small group. Finn was first and quickly named his weapon *"Lock Jaw"*, due to the questionable spring construction. Jury had to toss and turn all night long before he finally comes up with the imaginative name "*The Zeal of Zeus*". Julius was amazed by so much creativity and gave Jury a respectful glance. Max thought this was much too exaggerated and immediately made fun of it. In truth he simply couldn't pronounce it without stuttering and after some discussion he suggested abbreviating it with a practical *ZZ*. Jury was not enthusiastic about this, but the others convinced him that it didn't sound so bad. In contrast, Max had come up with the most inconspicuous name. He actually called his weapon *Music Teacher*. And in response to the skeptical and even somewhat shocked looks, he replied:

"When I use my grenade launcher on that thing, you'll get the joke."

After the ceremonial naming, which Flow sealed with another embarrassing blessing dance, the PvP rules and special tricks and tips of a Realgamer were discussed once again. This included various ways of moving across the battlefield, cover and shooting positions, as well as game modes. Zone Control (ZC) was obviously not new territory for the three of them, but there were still important things to consider here, which Julius drummed into them in clear terms. For anyone who doesn't know ZC, here's a short introduction:

Actually, it's quite simple. There are several zones in a defined area. Each of them is no larger than a few feet in diameter and is purely virtual. The teams must occupy these zones and if you go into the marked area, you need to wait a few seconds so that the team flag can be raised. The more player there are, the faster it goes. If you reach a zone that is already in possession of the opposing team, you must first remove the enemy's flag and put up your own. This means that you have to hold out a few seconds longer and, above all, survive. The following also applies here: The more gamers occupy the zone, all the better.

But that certainly wasn't everything. There was also a suitable armor for each mode and right coordination was also important here and Julius explained everything down to the smallest detail. He had specially selected and compiled some for the PvP games, which he now presented to everyone. First came the breastplates, then the arms and legs and not to forget the helmets. They were all mediocre quality, but still impressive in design. Jurys resembled an armored lizard, with a tapered "V" visor at the front. Finn's ran vertically upwards, as if he had a thick horn on his forehead. And Max's was more of a soldier shape, rounder and more functional. A Forrester banner was also engraved on each side, so that the armor could be carried around the square quite proudly.

A general weapon test followed. Everyone should learn to aim as quick as possible with their own gun and get a general feeling how to use it and to manage difficult situations. Of course, everyone immediately made a joke out of shooting at their buddy. And the harder and louder the bullets flew, the funnier it became. But amidst all the anticipation, the muzzle flash suddenly stopped as they got too close to each other. Max and Finn were already ranting that their weapon had a bug, but Julius explained that such close combat was not possible in PvP. Things were different at the beginning, so there were always bad clashes, and in order to avoid such things, everything had to be reprogrammed. From then on, weapons and abilities only worked in PvP mode from a certain radius that you always had to keep to your opponent.
This of course did not apply to virtual enemies, but only to real ones, with the intension everyone was forced to keep a certain safe distance and was not tempted to attack the player hard with body contact. The radius was only about some foot, but at least you should know that before you jump into battle. For this reason, Julius rarely used his sword in this game mode and instead swore by one of his Doubs. These were of course designed for long distances, but there were other questionable things that he insisted on vehemently and that each of the three had to internalize first.
For example, there was the combat mode and regulated the wearing of helmets. Normally, you could activate and deactivate it by pressing a button, which on the GG was located near the temple. If you activated it, you were particularly protected against headshots (HS) and generally strengthened your armor, but manually switching the helmet had its pitfalls, the extent of which you could not imagine as a newcomer.

There was a story about an incident where the enemy smuggled someone of the same stature and armor into the team. And since the face remained hidden under the helmet, a devastating grenade was thrown during battle. In one fell swoop, the entire team was wiped out and the match lost. That happened several times and for this reason, the activation of the helmets was strictly regulated, and it was precisely this regulation that Infinity's combat mode adopted. Once activated, the constant putting on and taking off a helmet was a thing from the past. So, if you were in a combat situation, you had it on. If there were no enemies nearby or the battle was finished, you took it automatically off. This gave you also a warning system as to whether there were enemies ahead. The only issue, what has to be mentioned, Julius added, was the short range. The mode could only detect enemies within a short, fixed radius.
"You should always be aware of this", he repeated and thus ended his lecture. Julius had to leave and was already too late for the first hour of class. Before he hurried off, he pointed his finger around the audience and handed his lesson over to someone else. This person stood up, crossed his arms puffing himself up and grinned dirtily.

Secret signs

Jury had already decided to avoid him of all the Forresters. He was talking about Pimkin. It was now his turn to teach the class and seemed to enjoy his new position of power, which Julius had given him with a simple gesture.
It started with him addressing the three boys as Stationgamers, rather than newcomers like the others. All of this with a certain aggressive undertone. Oh no, he practically shouted it. That was how he was. Whenever you wanted something from him or just asked a question, he made you feel inferior in some way, which was just annoying. Every contact felt like a ride on a roller coaster without seatbelt. You never knew what was going on in his head. Whether he hated you with all his heart and would immediately give you a thunderous blow, or whether he was just in a bad mood, and everything went just fine right the next day. If you weren't careful, this rollercoaster of emotions could rub off on you. Because if someone is always in a bad mood around you, you're get in a same mood as well and you start to think in the same way as him. Jury was annoyed by this, and of all these buddies, he was supposed to teach him something.
At first, you thought he was punching someone or putting them in a headlock. Perhaps he was using a special, long-honed technique, or how to deliver a good punch to the upper jaw without hurting yourself. But when Pimkin reared up and began his speech with "Shut up", you could really see the questioning faces of the SGs. I mean sorry, the newcomers.

The Forresters came up with crazy things to hide their plans in a battle. The enemy always wanted to know what the other was up to. Usually, each tactical move was communicated via voice connect, but since this could also be easily hacked using various apps, each clan had its own sign language. And Pimkin was the one who invented it. The three of them were already surprised

when they once observed Ox and Julius making strange movements from distance.
But it wasn't just the hands that were used here, the rest of the body was also involved in order to be able to transmit various commands and actions to a teammate. This was necessary because a lot of things were covered by armor and had to work even at great distance. Of course, all the signs weren't meant to be easy to read. That's why even simple commands were followed by a complicated sequence of movements that seemed very stupid when you imitated them for the first time. And the more extensive the action, the crazier it seemed.
Pimkin explained and little Tony performed the appropriate movements, which Flow then corrected if necessary. For example, there was a hold position. You stood with your legs apart, which called Pimkin the power position and then you raised one arm after the other over your head with a swing and as much rhythm as possible. Finn had to laugh out loud and immediately fell silent when he was asked to imitate it in front of the others. But he copied every movement that was shown to him perfectly, so that no one made fun of him as expected. Except for one, of course. Pimkin asked loudly around the group whether he should call a doctor, because Finn looked as if he had a big stroke. When he moved, it felt as if a huge stone was tied to his neck. So Pimkin immediately suggested a new name for him. "I know," he said, excited by his idea. "From now on, your nickname will be *Matn*. What does nothing mean anymore like: *Millstone around the neck*. And you will like it. Right?!" But Finn ignored this remark, which he found ridiculous, sat back proudly in the circle so that the lecture can be continued.

Next up was *the new zone*. Here you jump on the spot in jump style and pointed in the opposite direction with outstretched arms, which you spun up and down. *Stay in cover* was easier. You put your chin and arms firmly against your body, remained stiff as a board and turned around in a circle. This was followed by

Attack scissor 1, 2 and 3, watch out for snipers in position, Enemies coming from shown direction, and not to forget; *watch out for special attack*. Finn and Max also invented a few new ones in between. In particular they thought that Pimkin should learn these in the future as well. There were:
Watch out for a stone coming from unexpected direction. (here you look up aimlessly and stupidly), or *Eating Attack 2.0*, where you imitate a shovel that happily stuffs everything down your throat. *I'm not in the mood for that*, suggested Max. He casually swung his hips and waved his index finger in denial. When Pimkin noticed this little joke, he immediately started yelling again. You couldn't understand everything he was just about to say, but somehow you kept hearing one word, and that was:
"STATIONGAMER!!!"

But Pimkin didn't just attach importance to the execution. No, of course everything had to look as hip as possible and to ensure that the usual coolness factor was always maintained, he played loud music over each of the GGs. Dubstep, so as not to lose the grove, that everyone danced and grooved as much as they could. But all too often it happened, that the instructions were not followed, and some literally danced out of line. Then someone finally had a reason to freak out and that person screamed as loud as his voice would allow.
But actually, that wasn't bad at all. Because between the rattling beats, you wouldn't have understood him anyway, and at least he didn't get physical like he usually. Because strangely enough, the beat and the execution of the rhythmic movements seemed to somehow soften Pimkin, as if a snappy dog could only be tamed with music. The others also noticed that despite his fullness, there seemed to be a disguised dancer inside him, because he gave every movement that certain something. But what exactly these moves looked like, or how to imitate them, was really hard to remember. Even Finn, who apparently had a photographic memory in this regard, could only execute two of them. Luckily,

he wrote everything down right away and scribbled each move with a rough sketch in a small book. It was a worn notebook that he still had from school. You could read it on the cover in faded writing.
Everything what seemed important to him, Finn scribbled in it. He always carried it with him and thought that it made it easier to remember, but he rarely shared what was written down there. Finn liked to draw and so between the pages, which he filled with all kinds of notes and sayings, you could also find lots of sketches and funny faces. He had even sketched out the Grudge from the dare and Max and the Jury had to admit; It didn't look bad at all.

While Pimkin explained something about the fights, everyone sat back in a circle and listened. He showed how to move in the cover circle (CC). This method was definitely not a new invention, but extremely useful in combat, so everyone should get used to it. Finn eagerly wrote everything down.

The CC is always made up of several mates. They stand back-to-back, with everyone facing outwards and pointing their weapon. This creates a perfect attack and defense ring, especially in difficult terrain. Of course, there was also an order that everyone had to carry immediately when called out. Reacting quickly was just as important, otherwise even the best cover was pointless. While Jury tried to imagine everything that could go wrong in a fight, he noticed that Finn wasn't writing at all, but drawing. He grinned and scribbled hastily on one of the pages, which he cleverly covered with the opposite page. Jury looked over curiously. Finn had made a drawing of Pimkin. He depicted him as an overfat and sweaty garbage can, with small, cartoonish hands and eyes, he begged for someone to shit on him. He drew a speech bubble over it, which he now filled with what seemed to be a funny saying. Jury was not surprised by Finn's drawings. He had done that before. Rather, he was thinking. Because a small gust of wind made the pages of his notebook tremble, revealing a

few of their secrets for a brief moment. It wasn't just Pimkin he seemed to be ranting about, it wasn't possible to read everything because of all the scribbles, but there was even something about each of Forrester and Jury wondered if he had written something about him and Max as well to.
"PAY ATTENTION fu*kin SG," shouted Pimkin, his words hammering back into Jury's head. "For everything else, it's survival, duck, react quickly, adapt to the situation. That's it."
Pimkin had obviously finished his class. The Stationgamers should now use the time to practice and as soon as the others were back from family or fu*kin school, they should start immediately.

War Games

Little Tony climbed into a narrow, dirty pipe. It took only a moment for his tiny shoe soles to disappear behind a dark curtain of shadow.

Tony had the job of a spy, which he hated so much and let everyone know it right away. He even complained to Julius, but it didn't help, and every Forrester gave him arguments that were made up out of thin air.
"You're still too small," or "You just have to grow," they said, simply blocking out his loud complaints. Some of them also said less harmless things and made fun of him. But woe betide Julius who heard it, he would be hit right in the face.
Julius had a close, almost brotherly relationship with Tony. This was because he had picked him up from the grounds. He bailed him out, so to speak from a bad situation and has been almost half-starved, which is why he freaked out when Julius gave him one of his now beloved chocolate biscuits. At this time and young age, he strayed alone in the big city. So, he was also a real street kid, and the story was that he had burst into one of their games, and despite the fact, that the clan dropped important points that day, Julius had taken a liking to him ever since.

At this very moment, little Tony was crawling through a sewer pipe full of nasty insects. It was no big deal for him, because he had done it before his time with the Forresters. He moved quickly through the whole area like that. Yes, little Tony knew every hidden place and used paths that were no longer accessible to others. Whether under fallen steel beams, through rat-infested cellars or flooded supply shafts, little Tony always found a way to his goal. The Forresters, and Julius in particular, quickly noticed what made him special: An incredibly good sense of orientation.

For this reason, he had become indispensable to the clan and was tasked with spying on the enemy in today's zone control session. He carefully pushed himself out of the end of the pipe, shook the wildly crawling bugs off his hat and teased his virtual dog. He had to have him with him all the time and since Julius had given him this little app, he no longer felt alone. Because for a virtual fellow, it didn't matter which way little Tony took. Any living pet would probably have given up in fear after the first few dark shafts they had to crawl. Therefore, this program, this *buggy app*, as Ox like to call it, was the perfect buddy for Tony. Wherever he went, his virtual dog followed him.

Frolicking and playful, he hopped up a ledge next to Tony. Bright sunlight and a now opening sky promised a sweeping view. The ledge they climbed onto was formed from the remains of a multi-story building that was being demolished. At a long-disused intersection, it towered over the entire area. Nobody dared to climb up here. Too impassable and dilapidated it had been. So dilapidated that even a flyweight like Tony had to be careful where he stepped. Unexpectedly a chunk of concrete broke off nearby and crashed loudly into an abyss. Broken steel struts rose there like spears. Little Tony paused, looked down and let a thick drop of spit slide over his loosened lips. It took a few seconds until it splashed down. It was a frightening height, but Tony was unfazed and calmly petted his dog, who was vying for attention at a dizzying height, until a choppy voice rang out from his GG's ear studs:
"Li..ttle T..T.tony. Where are you?" It was Julius. He impatiently demanded an update on the situation. Tony obediently followed, crawling like a Pathfinder to the edge of the ledge and looked from right to left across the area that spread out before him.
"What's going on?" tactician Chris was heard asking with a yawn. "I can`t get any transmission from you, Tony." Chris had obviously already taken up his position and was waiting in a hiding place for the image signals from the Forrester.

As a tactician, you could actually tap into the perspective of your teammates. A practical thing, because this way, you could support each of them much more precisely and warn them of creeping enemies or give them additional tips. Positions were recorded using a map, which the tactician also controlled in order to maneuver the team through the respective tasks.
Chris was still complaining about Tony's poor image quality.
“Your signal is just too weak,” he called out tinnily, registering some traffic that did not belong to Infinity.
"You don't have your dog with you again, do you?", said Julius and asked him to turn it off. Tony, who was still lying on his stomach on the edge of the ledge, waved goodbye to his dog. The pet howled and growled once more and then literally vanished into thin air.
“Finally,” Chris was heard in a clear voice and since Tony had no more distractions, why he scanned the battlefield chosen by the tactician a little more closely. Suddenly he noticed something strange. Hidden behind a gutted Bus, an enemy player was running around and approached a virtual object. Tony started a new scan and couldn't believe his eyes.
“Hey guys,” he called out and waited excitedly for a response.
“What’s going on?” they asked at the same time.
"You won't believe it," he shouted. "The Assassins have a TOREX!"
Julius thought he had misheard and asked Chris for confirmation. But their spy was not mistaken. The enemy had a Torex and our three new guys, who were listening everything via voice connect, exchanged questioning gestures. Because none of them, even when they were Stationgamers, had ever had to deal with a Torex before. Whatever it was, it can't be that bad, they thought, and waited for instructions from the tactician, which they should be coming through their earpieces at any moment. Chris recorded the position of the Torex via Tony's GG and checked the countdown again. Because when it had elapsed, Infinity had synchronized on the servers and the game could begin.

Raging fire rained down on our newcomers. The three of them practically threw themselves into the flying projectiles. Not far from their position, they spotted an enemy zone and tried to approach it slowly. On the way there, however, the enemy fire became so strong that they thought it would be better to take cover and wait for the clan to support them. Luckily, Jury quickly found an old park bench, while Max and Finn crouched right next to it, protected behind a dented garbage container. But none of them were afraid or hesitant, on the contrary. Fascinated they noticed that the enemy defenses were striking next to them like they were teleported in a real action movie. The effects, sounds and everything else were visualized in such a perfect way, that the boys just had to laugh.
Of course, they had played VR many times before, but when you were under the glasses, isolated from the outside, things got too crazy sometimes and you quickly started to feel sick. That was different with augmented reality. The world you were in, was still the same. With the usual gravity, the air, and the weather, and all the movement had to make with your own body. All what the glasses did, was insert virtual content, born out of the developers' oh-so-active imagination. But in contrast to the dare, where the boys found themselves in a picturesque cave, there were no major changes in PvP. The battlefield was only sporadically enhanced with virtual structures. Here, the focus seemed to be more on the animation of the zones, flags, and banners, as well as extremely spectacular explosions, which thundered in numerous ways from every direction after the session was started. Completely harmless, of course. But once you saw conflagrations, burning oil drums and splintering wooden beams whirling through the air towards you, you automatically jumped for cover.
"Totally awesome," you could hear Max and Finn shouting every time something went bang and roared into the air somewhere.

You could easily take a few of the virtual bullets without being knocked out and if this happened anyway, your field of vision would darken, and a large message would loudly appear saying "you are dead". Of course, you could still follow the battle, but things like firing your weapon or similar interactions were logically deactivated and if you wanted to get back into the game, you first had to be revived by another player. They only had to touch the fallen one with their hand for few seconds and you could carry on.

Like so, Max had fun sticking his bare butt out of cover to take one hit after another. He did this until the health indicator lit up red. His GG wouldn't stop vibrating than.

Jury, Max, and Finn were having a great time. Their laughter echoed so loudly to the others that some of them let out an annoyed groan when the opponent scored another kill. The three of them knew that they had to make an effort, but the jokes of Max and his music teacher, with whom he soon had a real concert, were extremely contagious. Finn countered this nonsense with targeted shots in the enemy's face and when someone was careless, he shouted in an exaggerated voice: "Greets from Lockjaw" or: "That's what she said", and a lot more. When Jury heard it several times, he also began to comment on each of his kills accordingly:

"Be careful, it's me" or "Oops, you here too?" And suddenly, raging shots echoed across the battlefield. Even Pimkin joined in. During the fight, he roared in his usual manner and curses the enemy on every clanging explosion and went beyond all limits of good taste.

Each attack was accompanied by the filthiest of sayings. The others thought that was necessary to lure the opponent out of their shell. There was also a corresponding victory move to make it clear who was the better gamer. Everyone did that without exception and Jury concluded: Apparently another Forrester tradition.

They even had a term for it. They called it the *"PvP-diss"*. Finn especially enjoyed it and wrote something in his notebook. This time he shared it with his friends and read it out loud during a break:

It is considered good manners for every gamer to let out a diss sometimes. What it means: If you have made a good kill or elegantly escaped from a bad situation, you can use a rude move or saying on the person you have killed. This is completely fine and is received positively by most of the people. Now why is that? It shows that you accept your opponent as a real enemy and will not get lost in the crowd. But dissing, or GOOD dissing, is something you have to learn. But on the other hand, it is actually quite simple. A diss is only appropriate if it is justified. If you diss after easy kills or when you are in the majority, it turns negative. And such a cheap-looking provocation can drag the whole clan through the mud. So, an unwritten rule applies: If you diss your enemy, do it with decency and dignity. Then you are sure to gain the respect of all the gamers.

The Enemy

Their enemy were the *Assassins*. A team of Realgamer that Julius and the others had never mentioned before. There are seemed to be more player like the Forresters in this area. Gamers who had also founded their own clan, but where and how they lived was unknown, and nor was anyone supposed to find out. There was no friendship between the clans. No agreements, no easy contact. Another clan simply meant enemy, a competitor, a disruptive factor that had to be tamed. There was nothing more to it. No casual high-fives, no special interest, no bond. All there was envy, hatred, and amusement when the opponent messed up or wore ridiculous armor. The only thing Jury had to admit to himself was that the Assassins' banner looked very cool. Two middle fingers were visible on a striking purple background. The fingertips touched in the middle, forming a curved A. That had style.
Unfortunately, the Assassins' game was also impressive. Only with a few rather unintentional tricks could one or two matches be decided in the Forresters' favor. Jury also spontaneously slipped over his knees from cover to fatally hit one of the Assassins at the very last moment. That was the first time he had ripped his trousers, which he had worn long up until then, to shreds. And it wouldn`t be the last time, but the impressed look of Pimkin, who was cursing as he reloaded his weapon at that very moment, was enough reward for him.

In contrast to the Forresters, the Assassins mainly used magical weapons. This meant that they had to be prepared for sudden lightning storms, booby traps or even flying grenades.
Damn tricky beasts they were. Once caught, they would attach themselves insidiously and even could kill neighboring teammates. Only Flow was also able to use this technique.

Clearly, the assassins were good., damn good, so that every kill was celebrated extensively by more than just Jury, Max, and Finn. “Did you see that?!” was what you heard, demanding that your skills be appreciated and so were able to win some of their games, but when the Assassins used the Torex announced by little Tony, panic broke out in the truest sense of the word.
“You go out first.”
"No, you."
"No, you!"
"YOU..HU," argued Max and Finn, who had barricaded themselves with Jury behind a still-standing wall of the many demolished buildings. Little Tony also crept up and asked what was going on. Jury tensely pressed a finger to his lips and hissed: "Quiet", because between the usual tumult of battle, you suddenly heard powerful footsteps. Mechanical footstep noises, that seemed to be getting closer, so that everyone behind cover just flinched. Then they peeked through a hole in the wall, but nothing was to be seen. Only over VC had you heard the warning that Torex was walking across the battlefield and came closer to one of their positions, that every LL, or low life so to speak, should hide somewhere as quickly as possible. Little Tony was the only one who knew what to expect and so it didn't take long before everyone turned their heads in his direction.
“Let little Tony go outside”, Max said immediately. “Hey Tony, go and see what’s going on.”
"No way. I'm not a retard," he said and pressed himself between the boys.
The Torex was coming closer. You could hear it clearly and metal flashed behind cracks inside the wall for a few seconds. Suddenly there was silence. The boys moved closer together. A red light was approaching. It was some kind of laser. It was scanning the area like an insect with long feelers greedily searching for prey. The light was heading straight towards our gamers. Crawling across the floor, only a few inches to their toes. One after the other they slowly pulled their legs back, but it was too late. The

light continued up to their heads. Then it retreated and nothing happened. Everyone breathed a sigh of relief, as the Torex didn't seem to have noticed them.
But suddenly the walls shook. A huge machine reared up right in front of them and aimed two powerful missile slots directly at their faces. The boys were discovered and started screaming. There he was: Torex! Little Tony just said something like: "Okay, guys, I'm out. It's too OP for me," and fled. The others followed the suit. Jury ran. He made one turn after another. He jumped over walls, benches, and barrels, not distinguishing whether they were real or just virtual objects. That's what Julius had drilled into him. In between were the Assassins. They were constantly shooting at anyone who walked across the battlefield and after what felt like an eternity, Jury finally found a good position from where he observed something incredible.

The Torex was a killing machine like no other. At a height of minimum 15 feet, a tiny head was protected by powerful armor plates. Plates on which the banner of the Assassins was emblazoned, and which grew like a kind of collar from a V-shaped body that was carried across the battlefield by two massive legs. It moved mechanically and noisily, but Torex didn´t appear to be sluggish at all. Because when his legs did not move fast enough, powerful jump jets on his back helped out, which made him thunder across the battlefield like one of his smart projectiles. In addition, he was equipped with all kinds of tricky and bizarre weapons that a Realgamer could only dream of. Small mini cannons on his shoulders and arms that aimed in all imaginable directions. All the way up to a Gatling gun that fired about thousand shots a second. Every attack made a hell of a noise and his red eyes, which looked like fire slits in an iron Skull, wandered greedily across the battlefield, looking for victims. And you were a victim if this thing caught you. Torex not only had impenetrable armor, he also fired mini rockets from a severed forearm that reacted to movement and pulverized everything within a big. Yes,

even a butt as wide as Max's offered no defense. No attack, no matter how strong, everything was useless. Even Pimkin's insane battle cries like:
"Spinebreaker will melt you down," were of no use and when Torex moved towards the Forrester territory, tactician Chris was forced to reorganize the whole team. Julius and Ox defended the front. They apparently always did that, as their weapons and armor were the most powerful. But all they could do was distract Torex from weaker teammates and draw fire on themselves. Flow, Pimkin, and the others tried again and again to win the decisive zone for themselves with daring special attacks, but after countless attempts they failed. In such cases, a spy like Tony was helpful. Because if the enemy was sufficiently distracted and busy with an important goal, he could sneak up from behind and take over some zones as well. But since this was obviously not the first fight between Forresters and Assassins, they were prepared. Tony had failed hopelessly when he resolutely ventured into enemy territory under the cover of thick clouds of smoke. Even Julius, the strongest of all, wasn`t able to do anything.

Theory and practice

The days passed when the boys did nothing but fire their weapons, improve, and explore skills, and increase their XPs. So PvP ad nauseam if you will. But the three of them liked marathon-style gaming and Julius thought it was the best way to turn boring SGs into real RGs. By every evening they were exhausted and even before falling asleep they spent time finding the perfect match for their warrior setup. The good thing was that you could swap some of the items you received at the end of each match. Because some were just didn't suit your chosen class, or simply the type of weapon you had, so you need to test a lot of things out first and the best way to do that was in combat. That's why they spent whole afternoons to combat the Assassins as often as they could. This would work quite well if they hadn't had a machine called Torex. But luckily, they couldn't always use it. This cost resources of energy, and as soon as it appeared, you would hide in good cover if possible and wait until the danger had passed. Then you could concentrate on shooting easier targets again.

But sometimes everything was just too much, noted Jury. Hours of PvP, rushing, forming CCs, looking for good cover position and staying there, observing the terrain, spotting enemies, waiting for instructions, aiming, shooting, taking up the zone, moving on, keep shooting while moving on. Plus, walking, running, all that kind of shit. As a Stationgamer, you really weren't used to that. It was just exhausting and if you weren't wearing suitable clothing, everything was twice as hard.
Now they understood why the Forresters wore gloves and shin guards while gaming. They were truly helpful and protected from the inevitable injuries: scrapes, bloody abrasions, bruises. On top of that, each of them had sturdy shoes under their feet. Because the normal ones quickly just fell apart. From the laces to the

soles, there wasn't much left at the end of that day and the three boys tried to help themselves with duct tape, which they simply wrapped around at all broken parts. They even improvised a carrying strap in this way. Constantly carrying the weapon around could also become an annoying burden and so every evening they came up with new ideas to make the game easier, talked through mistakes they had made together and worked on their setup.

Dusk was already approaching in red clouds when the exhausted Forresters made one last attempt. The Assassins needed a dampener, or as Ox put it more aptly, they needed their ass kicked before the servers were shut down. He, Julius, and Chris went through the tactics again and motivated the others with the rule:
"Everyone screws up sometimes, but you never give up."
Even Jury had to suppress his hunger and thirst and looked hopefully into the faces of his friends. They also looked tired, and just as exhausted as he was. Finn in particular was longing for a break, but Chris assured him that he had something like an idea, a plan. He had thought of a way to defeat the Torex. The trick was a setup called *taser projectile*. Hard to get, but once you had it equipped, you just had to hit its tiny skull and then it was history. During the match, it had to be found somewhere on the battlefield and whoever managed to do so automatically had the honorable task of striking down the Torex. It is best for everyone to equip an aiming device to increase the chances of hitting the target.
"Let's go," Julius clapped his hands, encouraging the team one last time.

After the restart, Pimkin played one of his favorite songs in everyone's GG. To encourage the boys accordingly, as he said, so that the team went fighting during *The Prodigy – We live forever* was boomed in their heads. Everyone threw themselves into the battle and looked for that special item. Except for Finn, who preferred to stay on the edge of the battlefield. He just wanted to take things a little more slowly. Because at his position the countless explosions weren't thundering around your ears and Torex was also rarely seen in the narrowness of the dilapidated buildings. Between splintered windows and leftover household rubbish, he wanted to position himself in order to catch a few of the assassins from a distance. The admin had instructed him to always keep an eye on the Torex and to pass on every position of the enemy who dared to come out of cover. This time he left Jury and Max behind and preferred to move away from the action. Finn crept between broken remains of walls through a labyrinth of empty buildings. Suddenly, tactician Chris spoke up via VC. He asked him to go back the way he had come. Finn was surprised and Chris explained that he had seen something in one of the rooms. Then he turned around and went back again, while Chris kept giving him instructions.

"A little further to the left...or no, back again," he was heard saying. And indeed, after a few turns, both spotted a glowing object. A small box, golden-yellow in color. It was floating and spinning just above the ground. Chris literally went crazy and cheered so that the others could hear it too. The projectile had been found. But it was only the others who had reason to be happy. Too bad, thought Finn. Because the item was in a bad place. Like a shy bird, it was perched at the end of the room near a windowsill.

Although Finn was only a few steps away, but unfortunately there was a huge gap between them and the only way to across was above a dilapidated scaffolding of old wooden beams. The floor must have collapsed years ago, and Finn expressed clear doubts that he wouldn`t make it to the other side. Chris talked to him.

"You just have to be careful," he said calmly. "Just put one foot in front of the other." But Finn resisted.

"Forget it," he replied several times, and his fear grew up. Between all the wood, he didn't even know whether there were perhaps a few purely virtual structures hidden underneath. But Chris didn't give up and contrary to the admin's words, he assured him that everything that led over a hole was always real. "Oh, come on, you can do it," he encouraged him. "One foot in front of the other," Chris repeated, saying that no one else from the team was around. So, there wasn't much time left. He just had to take it and with item exchange Chris could equip the projectile by himself to finish off the Torex. Finn started sweating like crazy. Chris stormed off in the meantime and was already looking for a good hit position, while constantly asking how long it would take him. And when Pimkin yelled nasty things about VC, saying that all SGs were cowards, Finn started moving.

The wooden beams creaked. Plaster and dust trickled deep down, like a gorge that opened wider under his feet with every step. Finn spread his arms like an acrobat and carefully balanced piece by piece, further and further, until he only had to stretch out one hand to reach the small box. One more skillful shift of his body and he was done.
That was the theory. Now he just had to put it into practice and this time Finn exceeded his own expectations. He gathered all his courage, pushed aside his fear of height, and managed to do it exactly as he had planned in his mind. The projectile glowed brightly and popped into his inventory. Chris cheered:
"There you are. Now you just must do the following..." he immediately started talking, already tensely holding the Torex in his crosshairs. But at that very moment, Finn had other things to do. First, he wanted to get back safely and as quickly as possible, then he could happily give him the item. That’s why he didn't hesitate this time. But suddenly there was a roar and a crash. Chris immediately tried to call him, because his display suddenly went black, and just seconds later, a death of a teammate was displayed.

A worried voice was heard:
"Hey Finn, ...are you ok?" But no one answered. Chris immediately reported that someone should check on him. But this was not quite easy when there was no signal or position of the missing team member. Even Max and Jury had their difficulties in the chaos of the battle and searched in vain for Finn between the walls. Literally, this was the perfect time for the spy. He was the only one equipped with an extra-strong scanner. But Tony was on the other side of the battlefield and had to make his way all through where Finn was supposed to be. And with the mass of constantly attacking Assassins, there was no promise that he would ever reach his destination.

The ground had given way. However, despite his fear of heights, Finn had come a long way. But he lost his balance and had crashed with a loud bang straight down into the dark. It was truly a basement rat's nest. To his surprise, he had not been injured, apart from a few scratches and his knee, which seemed to hurt a little. But he was immediately out of action and thus taken out of the game. He tried to pass on his position via VC, but in Infinity that only worked if you weren't dead. Chris once commented on this topic with a now fateful saying: "Dead people don't talk," he said, and Finn only heard a mixture of fighting noises over the GG. None of the others knew where to find him when he tried to climb back, out of that rat hole. Furthermore, he had to find a teammate to revive him, because without the projectile there was no chance of defeating the Torex.
Suddenly he noticed movement in behind. Between the rubble and broken wood, he suspected that few tall Rats wanted to keep him company. But when he turned around, he frightened. An Assassin had suddenly appeared and pointed a weapon at him. He stepped out of dark shadows and stood there motionless. He wore a robe of amber colors and a long purple cape hung from silver shoulder armor, on which a wide-ranging drawing shimmered mysteriously. Through an equally impressively

decorated helmet the Assassin seemed to be staring at him. Based on the elaborate armor Finn concluded that he was at very high rank. Nobody said anything. Everything seemed to be frozen in time. Even the loud sounds of the ongoing battle had faded into the back. Finn still had one hand stretched up to grip it and remained in his position. The Assassin also seemed to be frozen. Finn had no idea what to think of and certainly not how to react. The enemy seemed to have seen through their plan and was now obviously trying to prevent him from returning to the game. Finn hoped that one of the guys would appear at any moment, to put an end to this awkward situation. But no one came. He then decided to open his helmet and fight the enemy face to face. Immediately after his visor disappeared, he said demandingly:
"Come on."
Another silent moment passed, and the Assassin examined his dirty and sweaty face, hidden under his helmet. Finn mentally prepared himself for a verbal duel followed by a fist fight. He gave his opponent a piercing look, clenched his fists and prepared a few of his worst insults. Then the Assassin moved and with a quick push of a button, he opened his helmet too. Finn immediately wanted to hurl a nasty insult, but all over sudden he fell silent. Under the helmet, and he couldn`t hardly believe his eyes, was a girl.

A death and a revival

Exhausted sighs and groans echoed through the headquarter. The Forresters took off their sweaty clothes and lit the big fire around which everyone gradually gathered. It was already evening and as Jury looked at the low sun, he noticed that gaming was literally eating up the day and wasn't the only one who had the same feeling. Hours must have passed without a sip of water or food, because inevitably after everyone sat down somewhere exhausted, their physical needs made themselves known. Max sprinted out of the SH, to disappear into one of the nearby bushes. In meanwhile Jury and Finn greedily shared a soda, where the carbonation was just as weak, only allowing a few isolated bubbles to rise.

Today's game was an outstanding success, despite the exhaustion that was now coursing through their bodies like a wave. While Chris kept his sights on the Torex from a safe distance, the others lured him into a trap. Hidden between walls, an opaque circle of Forresters formed and waited anxiously for the one shot that would change everything. Finn had surprisingly returned after an absence and was working on how to transfer the projectile to their tactician. From then on, it didn't take long, but patience was required. The killing machine kept bobbing out of its deadly crosshairs. Chris was sweating and had to concentrate. He only had one shot. One attempt to incapacitate the Torex. He took another deep breath, bit his lip and after a silent moment of tension, he pulled the trigger.
The machine began to stagger, valves hissed suspiciously, and the jump jets howled. Its weapons sputtered.
Some of the smart projectiles were still searching for targets, but soon it just fell to the ground like a lifeless stone. Torex massive body swayed from left to right a few times, then he collapsed like an empty shell without a soul. The power supply was disrupted.

Unfortunately, this only lasted for a few seconds, but that was enough time to unleash a concentrated firepower from the Forresters. Finally, the killing machine was defeated and so the enemy clan as well.
Even though you could still hear "damn assassins" throughout the room, everyone was happy with themselves and their performance. Visibly proud, they compared the loot they had earned that day. This included a few new weapon upgrades and class items. Every such as function and appearance were examined and discussed. Chris had now even received an attack bonus for combat machines, and while the headquarter filled with the smell of food roasting over a fire, the topic of Torex was picked apart in every detail.
A little way off, Finn had made himself comfortable in a corner. With his legs stretched out, he looked thoughtfully into his notebook. Ox came by and showed him a few tricks for battle. For example, how he could block a sudden attack with a simple sideways roll. But it was impossible for him to imitate it now.
In the meantime, there was a tumultuous atmosphere around the fire. Everyone was trying to get some food that Pimkin was mixing in a dirty pan from undefined cans and packages. He also had the job of preparing the food as a daily task and his combinations of beans, pasta with tomato sauce, plus undefined ingredients, were famous among the Forresters. Well, *famous* was perhaps not quite the right word, but his unusual creations, which were simply called *Pimkin's Allsorts*, were delicious and discussed very often and strangely always ended with a trip to the toilet.
Max poked Jury in the side and pointed at Finn with his bulging cheeks. Jury just shrugged and assumed that maybe he wasn't hungry or just wanted some peace after all. But Finn's sudden fall had probably left deeper wounds than he admitted. Even Flow noticed that as he tried to move into a more comfortable position and under the jeans, that were torn on one side blood dripped, staining the pants in a deep red. At that moment, Flow saw his

chance to finally prove his healing powers to the newcomers. Pimkin made an angry face at the fire, because in front of all hungry eyes Flow suddenly dropped his already filled plate on the floor and rushed over. Finn mumbled that it wouldn't hurt much and that it would somehow be fine. But Flow immediately talked about the possible options that promised a surefire cure for exactly such cases. Finn didn't like the idea and wasn't really in the mood to pay attention what a madman like Flow was talking about. But at least he was pleased that someone was worried about him and cared about his injury, which caused from the fall in that damn rat hole, so that he finally sat up and listened.

For example, there was the elaborate ceremony with the promising name *Warrior-back-to-life*. It involved an evening-long exorcism and promised a cure for life. But if something went wrong, - and that wouldn't be out of the question- his soul would be split into parts. Whatever it meant, the quicker version that Flow had on offer, was the orthopedically tested grip and twist technique, in combination with some effective healing curses. Finn didn't seem to be keen on any of these options and would have preferred an old box of prescription drugs, but to his own surprise he went for the latter. And while the others were still waiting eagerly for their food rations, an unprecedented healing was taking place in the background.
Every now and then you could hear Finn screaming, and everyone just turned their heads in his direction, with questioning faces. Flow said that he had to check that nothing was broken and lifted his leg in all directions. He mentioned almost casually that he couldn't see any blood and swore like a rough nurse just before retirement.

The treatment continued, so the rest of the clan preferred to focus on their food and the past match. Flow wondered how someone could get such a stupid injury from a ridiculous fall and talked about the fact that according to his display Finn was actually dead. Because nobody had revived him and he just showed up a little later, handed over the item and saved the entire game. Finn had told everyone that it must a been a bug because of his fall, but somehow Flow couldn't believe it. A tactician's display was usually never wrong, he said and continued his treatment while the others were still sitting greedily by the fire and didn't hear any of their conversation. For some reason Flow seemed trustworthy and so Finn reported what had happened shortly after his fall.

After the girl's helmet opened, Finn didn't move. He just stared at the unexpectedly pretty face, which was now getting closer. In just a few steps she had come up to his eye level and was looking at him. Suddenly she smiled and Finn flinched.
Because the girl touched him on the shoulder and only seconds were enough to revive him. In this strange moment, both of them let their gaze wander to the other and Finn was back in the game. But why had she done that? Why had she revived him? And instead of giving an answer, she just smiled and disappeared shortly afterwards, untraceable, back behind the winding walls and their dark shadows.

“Didn’t know that there were girls in the Assassins Clan,” said Finn, making Flow start laughing.
"Yeah, sure," he replied as if it were obvious. "The Assassins are all girls." Finn sat up straight.
“You’re kidding me, right? ...You mean, a clan full of girls?!”
"Yes," said Flow, "that's what happens sometimes." Finn wanted to really grill him, but out of nowhere, he said; that he didn`t want to talk about that and was now healed. Then he turned around on the spot and without any single more word, Flow went back to the others. Finn would have followed immediately, but his knee, which was obviously resisting any kind of healing, prevented him. He had no choice but to sit and listen to the conversation that followed. But one thing was certain, Finn

thought; Something here was fishy. Because why did Flow obviously avoid his questioning?
Angry words flew around, which in retrospect could be reduced to a simple one: Why did the enemy clan have a Torex? Well, the answer was simple, Julius took over. The Assassins had obviously successfully completed level number 11, because only there could you get this kind of loot. Everyone agreed as Finn listened intently, realizing that Torex wasn't the problem at all, but the fact that the enemy was already a step ahead of them. There were thirteen levels in total and the last three had to be completed before the event. After the tenth, there made a break. The school had been going through a time-consuming exam period, which inevitably forced some of them to study hard. The Assassins had apparently let this pass, so that the others now excitedly put their heads together and chatted among themselves. Because this deficit seemed to be a real embarrassment and Julius in particular had to struggle with it.
Jury and Max brought Finn something to eat and told him with wide eyes what the plan was. They wanted to get started as soon as possible. Julius and Ox had apparently had enough of wasting time. They wanted to get into the next Level without any delays. The tactician was already looking for a suitable place.
"Finn, did you hear that?" they called excitedly. "We're going into our first Realgaming-Level!" Finn nodded sporadically and they explained it to him in detail again. It was important to catch up as quickly as possible and this could only be done with the help of the next big step. Finn considered whether he should tell his friends that the Assassins were all girls, but the two of them were far too excited and talked non-stop, so he just swallowed everything that was buzzing around in his head. Maybe they didn`t even care about it and to the other hand, he had to digest this information himself first.

After everyone had more than satisfied their hunger, Julius called the Forresters together again. There was something important to celebrate after this successful battle. They stood in a circle and Julius wanted someone to step forward. Because this victory was certainly due to a special person who was crucial to today's success. Everyone put on their glasses and asked for quiet. Finn was still thinking about what would happen next. Whether he would perhaps be rewarded for his action, which was certainly dangerous and took its painful toll, so he waited spellbound in the circle. Jury and Max also looked at him in joyful anticipation. But to their and his disappointment, only one name was mentioned that evening and that was a tactician named Chris. Julius asked him to step forward and honored him with a shimmering medal, which he was allowed to wear on his armor from that day on. It was not just a simple badge, he explained, but also a signal for anyone who would stand in his way in the battles to come. An honorable symbol. A spear that breaks through strong armor in cracks that flashes with a silver glow, which declared its wearer as *Leader's spearhead*. The crowd went wild and admired his shoulder, where the badges he had won until its day were lined up on a wide-spread armored shield. Frustrated Finn went back to his usual corner with his injured knee and sat down there. Even the pitying pats on the back from his friends didn't really help him get over his disappointment and when the storm of enthusiasm among the Forresters had died down, Chris went up to Finn again. But instead of thanking him for the item he had brought, or perhaps offering a hand for good cooperation, he tried to explain why he had not been given this honor.

"Well,...having the item is one thing," he said, "but in the end, you have to get a precise headshot first," and quickly left so as not to get involved in a deeper conversation with him and preferred to be celebrated by the rest of the group.

Jury told him, he shouldn't care much about it and should rather concentrate on the next level. But Finn, annoyed by their loud waves of enthusiasm, withdrew and scribbled for a long time in his little notebook.

First try, last try

The next level was to be reached in the *First Try* (FT). That was the term used when you managed to get to the end without any checkpoints. In addition to the much-needed loot, you could also get an additional amount of XPs. With each restart, the value to be achieved was reduced and if the Forresters wanted to qualify for the big event, they had to make it in FT.
That's why it was important to find a suitable place where no one could disturb them. There were ideal places on the site, but the aim was to follow suit as unnoticed as the enemy had progressed. The assassins were not supposed to find out about it. The idea of launching a surprise attack with their own killing machine was too tempting. For that reason, Julius had given Chris the task of finding another location for the level. After another tough training session, the newcomers were not considered to be an impossible task and so it was a done deal that evening. The Forresters were geared up for attack and ready for any mischief. "Screw the Assassins," someone shouted, and in all the confusion, it was hard to understand everything that was flying through the SH, but the euphoria that things were finally moving forward was huge.

The guys talked about the dangers that lurked there. There was a talk of an ancient warrior race, shadowy forest dwellers who called themselves the *Kasales*. They supposedly had the ability, like the Sacoon, to appear without warning. This meant they could literally overrun their victims. That was all anyone knew. Infinity levels were different every time. They were also subject to the often-mentioned DP, or *dynamic programming*.
This meant that each environment changed according to its content, creating an exclusive experience. Everything there was some kind of theme that fit into the story. So, it didn't help to ask the ever-smart internet. It didn't spit out anything more than few

clips or images of the possible enemies, which they showed around in amazement.
"They're huge," said someone. "Hard to crack," said another. Nevertheless, everyone remained confident and before some of them set off for home, they discussed possible tactics and which special location would be suitable this time.

The training over the next days was okay, but still left a lot to be desired. While Jury and Max got on quite well from one lesson to another, Finn still had issues. Despite the efforts of a tireless magician, his injury just wouldn't heal, and he had to take longer breaks in between. Pimkin joked that Stationgamers had always been a bit weak, but when Chris started putting pressure on him too, an unexpected argument broke out.
He had only remarked that it would be better to leave a wounded man behind than to drag him across an entire level. That would only weaken the team immensely. He thus implied that Finn was probably not ready yet and suggested behind his back, that it would be better to go into the upcoming challenge without him. When Finn found out about this, he was angry. After all, Chris was also to blame for his injury. Because if he hadn't persuaded him to take a daring risk, he would have been ready for the last and important training. But the decision had apparently already been made. The admin had agreed to his suggestion via chat. The next Level should take place without him.

This put Max and Jury in a difficult position. Both would have preferred to go on strike and insist that without Finn there would be no level. But he didn't want that. Without a doubt, they would have been kicked out of the clan and the adventure would have come to a strait end. But the decision hit Finn very hard and soon left him limping sadly into a corner of the social hub. To calm him down, Jury said that they hadn't found a suitable place yet anyway and that there was still time to heal all his wounds. Max also talked to him, but when that didn't help much, he said:

"I have something that will take your mind off" and indicated that he will need his glasses and should come along.

Glaring sunlight shone down on Finn. Under a cloudless sky, he waded through a new area with Max and Jury. The city noise that had been constantly humming in the distance had disappeared. All that could be heard now was a gentle rustling. In distance, waving grass could be seen growing on golden dunes. A few seagulls circled above, and as Finn joyful watched their flight, one of them swooped down into a turquoise sea with a screeching sound.

Finn was amazed. A beautiful sandy beach suddenly spread out before him and behind the top of the hill, on which he was standing, the horizon filled with the waves of an unknown sea. Coconut trees lined the waterline. Where the water lapped vigorously at regular intervals, there was the sea as far as the eye could see. Only the beach marked a border. Jury and Finn were impressed. Then they walked on and followed Max, who was heading for a conspicuous spot. It was a rock where palm trees gathered, where the incredibly blue sea gently nestled around striking stones. He climbed up there and presented their new resting place with his arms outstretched.

Max had done a great job. Completely unnoticed, he had created a whole new world without their doing anything. The barren meadow of wild grass flowers had disappeared. The remains of the wall and concrete that had piled up to form a mountain of rubble were also just gone. Now, under their GGs, it had become a beautiful chalk cliff, on which the three of them sat together and looked out into the vastness of the sea.

Everyone knew exactly what he had used as a model. It was the image of his mother's postcard, which was recognized here. But no one asked why he had chosen this beach with its distinctive coconut palms. The two of them preferred to express their

admiration, marveling at the many details and the well-made animation of the surf.
But despite the beautiful sight, Finn was still upset. Both spoke kindly to him. In contrast to them he didn't like Julius. The same was true the other way round and was probably the reason why he agreed to Chris's suggestion without ever having been there for training. He was praised when he defeated the Torex and it's hard to believe that without Finn they wouldn't have been here as Realgamer at all. And now, he is the one who isn`t involved when they enter their first Raid.
Julius was a real asshole. Especially, when it came to Infinity, said Finn. Success was more important to him like anything and that's why he didn't want to play anymore and to become an RG. Maybe it was time to devote himself to other things than spending his time with the Forresters all day. He also missed gaming in their computer club *Alien* and the funny evenings on the top floor of their stairwell. But his friends had a pleading expression on their faces and certain inconsistencies, and the many unanswered questions were just bothering them too.
But furthermore, mentioned Max, he shouldn't forget where he still be. After all, this would be the land of the unbending and it is not yet time to leave it.
"Right", said Finn shortly and decided to get to the bottom of these questionable things before everything suddenly ended and to give the matter one last chance. Max and Jury smiled hopefully again as Finn said:
"Okay then, I give this dam story one last try."

School

Julius stared at the fibers of a wooden table. Next to it, a white sheet of paper with his name on it. A little further he had laid out a few pens and a cracked ruler. His chest was tight. He began to sweat between his fingers. The tension rose.

They were exams and the students squeezed between the extra wide tables to give evidence of the knowledge they had learned day after day.

Julius hated these moments. He quickly checked all the utensils again. In his head he went through one of the many tasks he had to make. In meantime, doors and windows were closed. The daylight and everyday noises were blocked out and in that very moment, he realized that he was a prisoner.

Nervous glances wandered, chairs and tables were moved into a better position. The minutes seemed to drag on longer and longer, until the teacher handed out the tasks, which were printed on threateningly colored paper, one by one in an arrogant step. This teacher loved the classic way of taking an exam.

Julius nervously ran his hand through his hair, nibbled on the end of his pen and read the questions laid out in front of him. If you don't understand a task straight away, you should move on to the next one, he thought, and was shocked to realize that he had already reached the last one after a short time, without having answered any of them adequately. All questions about history that is long gone. About days and people who lived long ago and who couldn't possibly have any more influence. So, that he not only didn't understand the tasks that had been set, but also their purpose. How was this kind of knowledge supposed to help him in the future? What damn use would it be in life, if he knew when and how someone in the past had lived and worked? He tried desperately to remember a few snippets of words from class. But

everything that had to do with it was too vague, too ticked off. When class started, he preferred to daydream about it, because when the teachers always started to talk, Julius thought of Infinity. He dreamed of the big adventures that lay ahead. The puzzles he hadn't solved, and the places he hadn't seen yet. And of course, the fame he could achieve. A glory that he could not achieve in the boring school.
If there had been questions on this sheet about which weapon and setup could kill a Grudge with a single shot, he would have happily answered it down to the last detail. He would have gotten an A+. Unfortunately, this knowledge was completely worthless for the school and especially for parents.

Unsurprisingly, the test didn't go well. So that the teacher asked him to come to his lounge for a small talk shortly afterwards. Julius had been looking forward to the break because he wanted to give a few instructions to his tactician which were crucial for the next level. But when a few boys annoyed him on the way with sayings like *cringe lord*, he thought it might be better to follow the teacher's words.

He sat down in front of a desk. Behind it, a man with a serious, worried expression. His teacher was talking to him. He had gotten so much better recently, and now this. Julius's scrawly handwriting and the many crossed-out answers on the test sheet waved in front of his face. In a few weeks are the final exams and according to this, he was in danger of failing again. His future was at stake, he was heard to say. His father paid a lot of school fees and how would he react if he failed again? Julius chewed a piece of gum, bored. Of course, he was worried about his future. After all, he didn't want to end up like a bum. Who wants that? But his idea of a fulfilling life fell apart between him and his teacher, and as he continued to talk, Julius' thoughts circled around.

A clear desire had taken root in him. He wanted to be successful at all costs. He just had to be persistent, and it would pay off eventually. Just like with every celebrity who was asked for their recipe. After all, he was the only one in his class, leader of a successful clan and well-known beyond that. No one else could say that about themselves. And that wasn't a coincidence, it was all thanks to his hard work and dedication. Not like the other students which saw gaming as just a fun way to pass time and quickly threw in the towel or lost interest when faced with some impossible tasks. For Julius, school was just a collection of those who dutifully did everything the people expected of them. Just to meet the standard and so school was just an annoying stopover for him. A necessary evil to please his parents, nothing more.

What felt like the hundredth test was a failure. Teachers who showed, warned, and knew everything better. You should be able to do this, you should be able to do that. There was talk, discussion and testing. The future was obviously a very important topic and only if you mastered the prescribed material, were you prepared for the great unknown. Julius felt that his own future had grown into something threatening. Like a burden that grew heavier every time an adult once again spread his wealth of experience over him.

He was trying to improve. He didn't want to disappoint his parents. But what good was fleeting praise if it quickly escalated into another pointless demand.

Contrary to what his teacher said, Julius thought a lot about his future. But school could only fulfill his vision to a limited extent. The event was his future. If he could pass there, he could do anything else. Because then people would know his name, then he would no longer be one of many. Anyone who didn't understand that could go to hell. Just like his stupid class teacher. Who has been doing his job well for twenty years without being nominated for Teacher of the Month once during this time, or any other higher office. No, he wanted to do everything

differently in his life and as soon as he was successful, most people would come crawling to him anyway. In contrast to him, he would stand out from the crowd and in an interview, he would only say good things about him:
“Yes, of course he was wild, but with a clear goal in mind,” he would say, smiling into the cam.
"Have you been listening?!!" asked his class teacher. Suddenly Julius was back in the room. Words of warning were spread that if he didn't improve, he would have to take actions that even he wouldn't approve of. A punishment so to speak. Whatever it was. Probably just cleaning up the entire gym again. Sorting balls and that kind of nonsense.
“Yeah, like last time,” Julius said mischievously when his teacher corrected him. The whole sports field had recently been closed for renovation work and the usual punishments would therefore be different. Perhaps he would think of some social project, he said, and Julius was taken aback. Not because of the serious look on his counterpart's face, but because of the little piece of information that had been thrown in. It made him think for a moment and then jump up.
“Perfect,” Julius shouted so loudly that his teacher flinched and then shook his head in dismay.
After the conversation, Julius left the room without saying a word. Before the door closed, his teacher pressed a few freshly printed pieces of paper into his hand. These were notices about the renovation that he was supposed to distribute in the hallway boxes. He complied without resistance because this time important information for him was also printed there.

Instead of hallway boxes there were also display boards for a while. Displays that made it easier to distribute short-term information to everyone. But this also made it easier to hack these things and so it wasn't long before someone posted not only fake and false reports but also the usual filth from the internet. Sex education in brief, someone jokingly added. A temporary worker had to react quickly and cover everything with paper to avoid a class action lawsuit from angry parents. Thus, these things quickly became out of fashion and, as the headmaster explained in a statement, they relied on the tried and tested again.

Students ran wild through the corridors. They laughed and made the typical noise when you are released into freedom for a short time after class. Julius was ignored, pushed a few of the annoying kids aside and only at the last information point did the usual stupid comments follow:
"What does it say? The sports field is being renovated. It was about time. I fell into a cow-deep hole while playing football the other day." Then laughter and so on. Suddenly it hit Julius like lightning. Next to his information sheet and notes for other activities, there was another one, that immediately caught his attention. The school bell was now ringing shrilly to end the break. He carefully took it off and read what was written in a large heading.

Ran away!
Concerned parents search for their child.
Who has seen this boy? Please contact the office.

Underneath was a photo of Jury. Julius didn't pin the note back, however. He looked around. The students ran back to their classrooms. No one paid him any attention. Then he crumpled up the paper and quickly hid it in his pocket.

Obstacles

"And you really think that's a good idea?" Ox expressed his final doubts and crossed his arms. But Julius and the others were convinced.
The Forresters stood in front of a long wire fence. Signs hung in every open space, warning of the dangers with ominous symbols. Behind it was an old school with a sports field and drab bleachers, where wild bushes grew, obscuring a view inside. Renovation work was underway, and no one was around during this time. For Julius and Chris, the perfect place. Exactly what they were looking for. No one would notice their activities here. The fence was high, but not insurmountable in some places. So, it didn't take long for Julius to take the first step. The others followed. One after the other, like a chain, the Forresters climbed. Even little Tony, who was supposed to have more difficulty, wasn't bothered by it. Quite the opposite. After his legs reached the other side, he made a skillful jump. Jury and Max were last, letting the others go first. Climbing fences into forbidden areas had never been an issue for them, but both were still a little unsure. Because now things were getting serious. Did they really have what it takes to become Realgamers? Could they even keep up with all the levels the others had already completed? All questions that occupied their minds at that moment. Sure, each of them had become a member of the clan by now. But were they truly accepted? Joined into the club with all their quirks and peculiarities? That obviously wasn't the case with Finn, and Jury, in particular, was struggling with it. Because between the funny conversations around the fire, there were still the occasional vague glance that cast doubt on that. But there was no time for worried thoughts, said Max, ending the conversation with one of his usual gags.

"Parents are responsible for their children," he read aloud on a sign. "Well, that's fine with me," he added with a grin and began climbing. Jury followed him.

The ground was uneven and cracked. Drains clogged with rain debris. A vast expanse of ground lay before them. In the middle of all was the sports field. More like a trampled meadow with soccer goals and a running track around them. The white marking lines were faded, the railings rusted. No one was to be seen. Even in the stands, it seemed as if no spectator had sat in the plastic bowls and cheered on someone for a long time. While some looked around with interest and rummaged through some of the building materials stored there, Chris searched for a suitable place to enter. Jury wanted to know everything in detail and kept an eye on him. Fortunately, this time he was well-rested. He was in a good mood and explained everything he wanted to know. Chris took out a can of spray paint and painted the symbol of the eleventh level in red on the floor in front of him. A circle with a complex symbol inside that Jury couldn't possibly remember. It looked like a pentagram with numbers. That was the starting point, and everything else that happened in a level inevitably depended on it. At least, those were his words when Jury asked them to double-check the necessary equipment. After activation, there was no time for that, and as soon as things started, the admin had sole control. That was important, because from then on, he assumed sole leadership and responsibility. As a tactician, you also had a lot to say, said Chris, but it was more of an advisory role, and the final decision on what to do always lay with the Leader. Jury nodded, and Julius called everyone together. Then the boys put on their goggles and scanned the symbol.

A wall of polygons rose up before them. It stretched ever further across the square, with the individual stones clacking together loudly, only ending at one of the adjacent fences. It looked like a fortress, with the entrance forming right in its center. A huge

gate. Round, closed, decorated with golden curls of mystical symbols and resembled the dial of an antique clock. But instead of numbers, various symbols could be seen, which apparently represented the thirteen levels. Golden symbols, presented in countless variations, lines, and shapes in an intricate manner. One of them stood out from the others. Placed in the center and larger than all the others. It must represent the number 11, and where the flourishes met at a point, one could make out a kind of keyhole. So, behind it lay the level. Or, among gamers, also called *Raid*. The great adventure that everyone eagerly awaited.
While Jury kept his distance, Max observed the bricks, which gradually fitted together almost magically, and remarked that this structure reminded him of something from a famous fairy tale series. Chris nodded understandably and, somewhat metaphorically, mentioned that many things repeat themselves in games and their stories.
“Only in contrast, this is not fantasy, it is reality,” he said. Artificial or virtual, no matter what you called it, this structure somehow existed on the servers and thus had every right to exist.
"All well and good," Max chimed in, still wondering how an entire level could open up behind it. Curious, he wanted to poke his head through to take a look at the other side. But Julius held him back. This wall was a boundary that was not to be crossed. It was still just a virtual construct where nothing happened. But once you went through the gate, you were registered as a participant and the game began, he warned. Therefore, he should definitely not do this within these walls, as this would mean instant death for the gamer. The system recorded the positions of every teammate, and as soon as someone left the designated area, they were automatically excluded. In other words, kicked from the game. But like every level, this one also had to be activated first. Chris's tag only determined the starting point. Therefore, at this moment, there was nothing inside this fortress other than the sports field. Activation opened the gate, which was only possible with the corresponding key, of course. Only then could

the level become clear. Nevertheless, Max wanted to see for himself that all the teachings were correct, and since he was always quite stubborn in such matters, Julius agreed and let him have his way. Therefore, Max looked through, and when he turned back shortly afterwards, he said:
"I'm not sure if this is a joke, but there's someone behind it."
Julius cowardly.
“Good joke,” he said, saying that the others joined in.
"And who exactly is that?" shouted Pimkin. "Already the final boss, or how.” Everyone laughed.
“Then take a look for yourself,” replied Max, and only when the seriousness in his voice was heard did everyone excitedly run to the wall and stick their heads through.

Meanwhile, one member had stayed behind at HQ. He was still crouching on his sleeping berth, scribbling in his notebook. It would certainly be some time before the others returned from their mission, so he was passing the time in this place to relieve his boredom.
Early that morning, Finn had already made a decision. One he considered best. His knee was feeling better, and before he finalized his decision, he took one last look around. Thoughtfully, he glanced into the armory, which seemed completely empty. Only his cobbled-together piece, his Lock Jaw, and the unusable, broken things remained. Just like him, Finn thought, and sighed at the fact that even the annoying nickname of Pimkin now suited him. One that he occasionally called Max, depending on the situation, but which ultimately stuck with him: *Matn*

He tried skateboarding for a while, then a few basket shots on the pukeball court, before putting on the GG and marveling once more at the creatures' glass containers. Each level seemed to contain a world of its own and its residents, with ever-changing environments, experiences, and tasks. And so, he wondered what incredible things they might see this time, from which he was excluded.

Finn had to distract himself and subjected everything that caught his eye to careful scrutiny. At the door to the throne room, he turned the handle again. Unexpectedly, it swung open. In fact, for the first time, Julius had forgotten to lock it. Probably because of the chaos of the last few days. But as expected, the surveillance drone swooped in at the same moment and began its usual fuss. Finn tried to stand his ground and make it clear that he was also a member of the clan and therefore had the right to enter. But this arrogant thing insisted on turning off everything inside the room, as required by the protocol imposed by the Admin. Finn shrugged indifferently, took off his GG, and entered the room.

The throne room had lost all its splendor, and everything that had once shone brightly and brilliantly in this space was gone. The perch, where only the admin was allowed to sit, was nothing more than an old chair with tattered backrests, propped up on dilapidated wooden pallets. Finn climbed up and sat down. But without the GG, there was nothing of interest or note here. Just a few dirty clothes, cobwebs, a textbook on the bygone Roman Empire, and a skateboard repair kit. Nothing else. Behind it, small, screened windows.

Finn spotted a drawing on the wall. Without his glasses, it probably would never have come into focus, and it took him a moment to recognize some kind of diagram. Somewhat hidden Behind the seat, it had been carved into the crumbling masonry. Mainly squares and circles, connected by chalk lines. One could recognize something like symbols and shadowy faces in it. Abbreviations underneath. But he couldn't understand them. Disappointed, he left the room and spent his time doing other things. He devoted himself to rummaging through the trophy cabinet, examining each individual piece. He was particularly fascinated by the creature from the Valley of Dreams, which looked like a magic bird. When touched, it flapped its wings wildly, emitted a timid screech, and dug its claws deep into the metal base. A base that could rotate, and the winner could be read in a shiny engraving. The name *Forrester* was written there, and below it, an additional note:

earned by Assassin Girl

Finn paused. So there had to be some kind of connection between the clans. But which one? Whether that would ever be discovered was just as doubtful as the question of being successful in this clan. Finn took out his notebook and looked at the drawing he had just finished. It was the face of the girl he had clearly seen in his last match, and so he wrote a name underneath: *Assassin Girl.* To remember it and not forget her anytime soon. Then he went back to his sleeping place, put down his glasses, and packed his backpack to set off. Back into the hustle and bustle of the city. Back into the deep canyons of the urban jungle.

Sure, he'd told his friends something different. There was talk of a *last try* recently. Maybe he was just trying to lull them into a false sense of security. But his mind was made up. If they went on the raid without him, he wouldn't have to stay any longer. They'd understand and would probably do the same. They'd be fine without him. After all, they'd had to do that before they met, too, and this was the perfect time to slip away unnoticed. Without any stupid goodbye. Because for Finn, it was time to make his way out on his own again. And to appropriately emphasize the end of his life as a Realgamer, he left the glasses in their holder. Their tracking would have made him quickly traceable. Besides, it wouldn't be okay to take a device of such value with him. So he left Forrester headquarters and quietly made his way.

In fact, there was actually someone in the middle of the football field. While the fortress wall was being built, someone had apparently crept up unnoticed behind it, put up a parasol, and placed a camping chair in its shade. It was a woman with a big sun hat and glasses. She wore a light blouse and tight trousers, which she had rolled up to her pale calves because of the heat. She reached into a bag and started applying sunscreen. The scene was so strange that everyone watched it silently for a while and it wasn't until Pimkin let out a loud "F*CK" that anyone realized what was going on. The woman elegantly took off her glasses and looked over at them. She seemed to have expected this situation and started laughing so hard that it sent shivers down your spine. So that was her.
"Eggersfeld," Pimkin hissed for everyone to hear. Jury would have expected someone with a perfectly updo, horn-rimmed glasses, and a tight-fitting pleated skirt. Just what you would imagine a teacher to be like for boring lessons. But this woman, with her rather casual style of dress, didn't fit the image he'd created at all.
Her intention for being here at this very moment was clear. She wanted to spoil their fun, and unfortunately, they all had to admit, she was easily able to do that. Now it was impossible to go through the gate if there was someone uninvolved there. This was clear to everyone and she seemed to enjoy this fact to the fullest when she said shortly afterwards:
"Well, who do we have here?", as if she'd just caught the boys in the act of committing a serious crime. " All truants actually in one

place. I guess today is my lucky day," she said spitefully, and only then did Max and Jury recognize her distinctive voice. It was the person they'd first tried the heel-ripper on in the shopping mall, and now she was standing unexpectedly in front of them. The city was sometimes frighteningly small, Max whispered, while Julius loudly defended himself.
“But there is no school today,” he said, wanting to know how she could have even known about it.
"Well, instinct, my dear," she replied arrogantly, adding that they should also be careful what they were posting all the time. Because that way, everything would be easy to find out. Julius was the first to take off his glasses in frustration, so that their plan to get to the level had a finality for everyone at that point.

Mrs. Eggersfeld talked about how she'd been specifically assigned to sabotage their game today. Their client? Concerned parents who were doing everything they could to bring each of them back to their senses. All of this would be a terrible waste of time. Especially now, with so many tests and exams coming up. After all, the other students would have their heads engrossed in books at this time, not playing a pointless game. Especially in a dangerous place like this, she began to list in panic:
"With the holey floor, the unsecured stairs, and downright deadly construction equipment." She didn't want to imagine what could happen there, and gave everyone a long, drawn-out lecture after she came over. With her nose in the air, she strutted past, casting a disciplinary look at every opportunity. "What do you think you're doing to your parents?" she sighed, then raised her tone and volume. "ALWAYS STAYING AWAY late! Without SUPERVISION, without CONTROL. Everything's getting out of hand. What will become of you?" she lowered her voice again to feign sympathy. "If this continues, you'll end up in the gutter. And all this just because of one stupid game? By next summer, it'll all be forgotten anyway, and then what? Then your life will already be lost. Especially you, Julius, from whom so much is expected.

Your father—a truly sympathetic man—is very worried. Your mother also wrote to me PERSONALLY to stop you from doing such crazy things. So it's only for your own good. The same goes for you, Klaus, by the way." Max and Jury exchanged questioning glances, because Mrs. Eggersfeld had stopped in front of Ox and was looking for eye contact.
"Klaus Kattowixz! I'm talking to you!" she yelled. But Ox didn't need to reply because someone immediately started laughing out loud. It was Max, who couldn't hold back any longer. Even a tear rolled from his eyes and he was gasping for air. She, on the other hand, didn't find it funny at all that she rushed over angrily and gave Jury a hateful look too. "I don't know you," she said thoughtfully. "You don't go to this school. But you all seem familiar to me." She noticeably licked her lips and let more than a few drops of saliva fly in their direction. Apparently, she had an unnatural problem with salivation. Some people just had it. Especially when they were really upset.
Jury didn't reply while Max tried to pull himself together. Then she marched back to the others and ordered them to follow her so that they could be picked up by their parents, and of course, there would be a proper consequence to all this. Her answer to this misstep: school detention. With that sentence, someone suddenly had enough and started running. It was Pimkin, who couldn't control himself any longer. Faster than expected, he ran back to the fence, and the others didn't think this was a bad idea at all. Because what was she supposed to do? Mrs. Eggersfeld was still hissing like a wild cat, but it was too late. Everyone was running in different directions, so she couldn't follow. Two disappeared over the fence, another into the bushes. Someone else crawled between the seats in the stands and Jury followed little Tony, who discovered an unlocked door to the locker rooms.

Continue

"Come out, come out. I know you're here," Eggersfeld could be heard yelling through the halls like a freak, and Jury sprinted into the girls' restroom, hoping she wouldn't look there. He hastily stepped onto one of the toilet seats inside the stalls and leaned behind a partition. Then he heard the squeaking of shoes. Footsteps which getting closer. Jury tried not to breathe, sliding slowly further over the edge of the bowl. He had to hold on with all his might. Suddenly, someone peeked around the corner. Jury flinched. But luckily it was only little Tony, who, like him, froze for a brief moment. Jury waved a hand and indicated that he should find another hiding place, because two in one place would be far too dangerous. As Tony obeyed and disappeared from the restroom again, Jury realized that, unfortunately, there was only one way out. He'd be trapped if she showed up here. And maybe nothing she said was true. After all, she was a stranger. And maybe everything was completely different. Because there had to be some other reason why Pimkin was so afraid of her. Perhaps she wasn't even a real person, and only when it was too late would her true self reveal itself.

Eggersfeld would transform into a snarling monster. Her pale skin would burst open like a dead shell, revealing a black, slimy alien beneath. With a massive maw, greedy eyes, and long, bony claws instead of hands. One that hadn't eaten in ages and was thirsting for blood. Fresh blood.

Clearly, he had to get out of there. So he ran back into the hallway, carefully looking around every corner. There was no one in sight, not even Tony. Group photos of students hung on the walls, and as Jury tensely looked in all directions, he happened to recognize a few of the Forresters. They were Ox, Julius, and Chris, who were apparently in the same class or played on the same team and had met there.

Suddenly, the sound of a door opening. Jury crept into the next room. There was no good hiding place here either. Only lockers, benches, visible on all sides. The light flickered and approaching footsteps could be heard. Nervously, he stared at some of the metal lockers, wondering if there was any way to squeeze in. Suddenly, he was startled. Because the very first one he opened was Tony, crouching. Tony waved a hand and whispered, as Jury had just minutes before, that he should find somewhere else, and then closed the door forcefully. The sound made the footsteps quicken and shortened the time left so that Jury tried the next one straight away. But he couldn't do it without putting his weapon down. He quickly pushed it up onto the locker and, before anyone entered the room, squeezed in and quietly closed the small door.

Jury watched the room through the air vent. A shadow approached, apparently checking each of the lockers for its contents. Tense, he closed his eyes, only then to realize that this person was more dangerous than any final boss that awaited him in the raid. Just one careless moment was enough. It would be unthinkable if she caught him. She would find out everything, tell his parents, and then the adventure would be over in an instant, without him ever having seen a single one of the incredible levels. And there was no checkpoint to restart from. No continue or save. Even the weapon was useless here. All the preparation was completely in vain. Because even the most powerful Infinity upgrade wouldn't have been able to do anything.
What a tricky situation. Not the first one requiring courage and patience, of course. But unlike those ones had to master in games, one that couldn't be postponed.
Eggersfeld searched and rummaged. Jury didn't make a sound and tried to make himself small. He could only see a tiny area and thus could only guess where she was. Suddenly he heard a horrible noise. It was as if a strange being were in the room with him. One that was breathing greedily, even wheezing. A terrible

shudder ran through Jury and felt his legs becoming increasingly numb. Mrs. Eggersfeld now came into view and he hardly dared to look because her breathing sounded simply horrible. She also became more and more hunched over, while practically drooling. Mucus dripped. Jury sensed something bad was happening and, amidst the constantly flickering light, he squeezed his eyes shut in tension until she unexpectedly pulled out an asthma inhaler and inhaled deeply.
"Ahhh, this damn pollen season," he heard her sniffle, and, "Ouch, this damn folding chair," she held her back, switched on the light and complained that nothing was working properly. Then it wasn't long before little Tony was being pulled out of his hiding place by her. She dragged him towards the exit with lecturing words and just when Jury thought he had gotten away, she stopped and went back again, cast a suspicious glance into the changing room and switched off the light. Jury took a deep breath. Apparently, she had only seen Tony come in here and still thought it best to wait a moment until suddenly two glowing eyes stared at him through the ventilation shaft.
“Now I have you”, one heard Mrs. Eggersfeld and with one leap she tore the locker. Her grip was so tight that at the same moment something fell from above onto her head. It was Jury's gun. A scream thundered through the locker room, forcing him to break free and sense his only chance. He quickly jumped away and ran back to freedom.

Jury quickly climbed over the fence. He looked around nervously. Luckily, there was no one in sight. No annoying substitute teacher, or anyone else calling themselves a chaperone. But unfortunately, none of his mates were anywhere nearby either, and to make matters worse, he'd left his weapon behind. He'd had to sacrifice it in the heat of the moment, so to speak, and planned to retrieve it when things calmed down again. So he waited. Because sooner or later, one of his mates was bound to

show up, and going back there alone wasn't a good idea for him either.
But to his surprise, even after a while, no one came, so he tried to reach Max on the GG. But there, too, no answer, no reaction. Jury called everywhere. His team had practically dispersed in such a short time, like a flock of startled city pigeons, and each of them seemed to have taken a different escape route. No one answered his calls. Julius's refusal to say that the raid was officially called off also went unanswered, and in the short notice and urgency, no one had thought of a plan B, which is why he even tried to reach Finn. But that also failed.
Strange, Jury wondered thoughtfully. Surely it would be advisable to return to HQ as quickly as possible, which the others were most likely aiming for as well. But without his ZZ, which he desperately needed, that was out of the question. Besides, the sports field where they had gathered was a considerable distance away. Impossible to reach on foot, so a ride or train was unavoidable. But Max had pocketed the ticket he always forged for the free rides, and Jury didn't know how to do such a thing. So he waited another half hour, observing the entire place, hoping to see someone leave. But nothing of the sort happened, so after an agonizingly long wait, he wandered around a bit. Apparently, some strange characters noticed this, and someone in dirty clothes and a scratchy voice asked:
"Hey kid, what are you doing here?" And when the guy began to follow him with short steps, Jury was driven away. Deeper and deeper into the blind streets of concrete houses.
Rather, he had gotten lost along the way. He turned into one of the many winding streets and tried everything to reach his friends. But nothing happened. All his devices were apparently switched off or blocked, and he tried to calm himself with the thought that someone would get in touch eventually. But the more time passed and the more unanswered messages failed to arrive, the first concerns arose. Worried thoughts that it would probably take forever to reach HQ on foot and alone. He had

packed some provisions in his backpack, as planned for the raid, but even that would only last so long. The many strangers wandering around suddenly overwhelmed him. The noise of the big city roared. There was hustle and bustle everywhere: cars, shops, vehicles. Even the distinctive sound of the rotor blades of several helicopters could be heard. Engines that cut through the heated air like knives and circled the sky like an attacked wasp's nest. And there were the sirens of ambulances and police.
Before him stretched an unknown territory, and on this day, Jury was certainly prepared for something other than wandering alone and lost through such a destructive environment. And as he desperately tried to orient himself on the GG map, even shaking off clingy figures, an idea suddenly occurred to him.
When the unexpected happened, Max said, there was always a place where you could meet again. Of course, thought Jury. The meeting point! As it happened, it wasn't too far away, so he headed there right away.

He repeatedly tried to cross the street between traffic and what initially seemed like a ridiculously paranoid fear soon turned out to be an unpleasant truth. The strange guy he had initially encountered didn't let up and followed him as inconspicuously as possible. An uncomfortable fact that could no longer be ignored. Therefore, Jury quickly packed the GG back into his backpack and set off purposefully towards his new destination, ready to seek refuge there for a while if necessary.
The kiosk, perched on a triangle of buildings, still sold the same things: an assortment of drinks, tobacco, and news from all over the world. The scantily clad girls still hung behind its dusty glass, leering. Even the owner seemed to be wearing the same clothes, as if not a spark of time had passed between their last visit. Simply nothing had changed, which was certainly reassuring. However, here, too, all one could see were the many busy people flowing inexorably past like a bubbling stream.

Searching for Max, Jury scanned the crowd, and after climbing to their usual elevated position on the bridge as usual to get a better view, he spotted the man again, who had continued to follow him and was looking around searchingly. Jury wasn't sure what he wanted from him. But he wasn't interested in finding out, and suspected that, like so many impoverished residents of this city, he had been lured by the glasses, which he had worn around his neck for a while like a luxurious piece of jewelry. Even Ox had warned against carrying such expensive equipment around openly. But with all the exertion of the last few hours, such things were quickly forgotten.
In any case, he thought it better not to keep watch high up on the ledge, but to wait for him under the cover of the thronging pedestrians. This would make his search more difficult, but minimize the risk of the guy spotting him as well.

A gruelingly long time passed, with Jury scanning the crowd and immediately retreating back to it so as not to attract attention. Because, as crazy as it may sound, it seemed that there wasn't just one person searching for him anymore. Shortly afterwards, the man apparently brought a friend with him, who also literally searched the streets for him. Jury didn't understand what was going on, but one thing remained certain: he had to be careful. So he continued to look out from the cover of the crowd, and the situation probably would have dragged on forever if someone hadn't nudged him from the side. Startled, he stepped back. But it wasn't a stalker or a stranger. In fact, standing there, right next to him, was little Tony. Jury was super happy to see a familiar face again, although at the same time he wondered how he managed to track him down there completely unnoticed. To which he only replied with a biting remark:
"I'm a spy," he said, and recounted his equally successful escape from the sports grounds. Only he'd come out the other way, and Max had asked him to stop by.

Jury immediately expressed disappointment and wanted to know why he hadn't come himself, and why no one had responded to his messages. Tony simply responded curtly that he shouldn't get so worked up, because it was simply impossible, and pulled him by the hand into the crowd to escort him to another meeting point, as instructed. The nearest train station was the new destination.

But Jury refused. He didn't want to go back without his ZZ. Tony reassured him that Max had tracked it down and taken it, without failing to mention that it wouldn't be a good attitude for a Realgamer to just leave it lying around somewhere. Jury obeyed and, given this hostility, didn't think it worth mentioning that, for some unknown reason, he had a few shadowy pursuers. This turned out to be a mistake. Because a little later, when they stopped at an intersection, two washed-up guys stood behind them and suddenly tried to grab them. Tony had no idea what was happening, but he managed to free himself from their grasp and immediately took off running, right through the traffic. Jury did the same. He jumped over a braking car hood and then crashed loudly into a barrier that directed traffic into fixed paths with flashing lights. Cars honked. People looked around. Jury tried to explain the situation while still running. But what could he have said if he didn't even know it himself? But Tony didn't listen and kept running.

Passing pedestrians, construction workers, fruit vendors, and garbage collectors. Like in a shit fu*king kung fu movie, Chris would say, both of them tumbled over obstacles. They dodged fruit crates, parcel delivery men, ringing scooters, mopeds, bicycles, and fat women. They jumped under and over people who were carrying goods or standing just in the way. Even the pet dog of a distinguished walker broke free and ran after them, barking wildly and whipping its leash across the ground. And when another, larger dog noticed this, he joined in as well - true to the motto: *A damn fresh meat hunt?! Of course I'm in.*

Jury was angry with the owner, asking why they couldn't control their dogs while they threw the same thing back and complained loudly about the careless running around. But this didn't distract their pursuers. Quite the opposite. It actually kept them on their trail.

At a bend, Tony finally stopped. And while he was there, breathing heavily, searching for the right turn, Jury, just as frantically, was searching for clarification. But to his surprise, he didn't have to explain himself to him. There was no need. Because as a street kid, you were, I don't want to say used to such situations, but they were familiar. For either of them, it wasn't the first time they had had to assert themselves against aggressive characters, and equally nothing new to have to extricate themselves from difficult situations like this. Therefore, no explanation was needed, and what they wanted wasn't important either, because it simply couldn't be anything good. "This way," Tony called, urging Jury on through the maze of streets and realized with amazement, that Tony knew his way around. He didn't even need to check an app when, as announced, he disappeared through the open door of a foreign fast-food restaurant and fled through a narrow hallway, first through the kitchen, then through a backyard with sleek clotheslines and another exit with a heavy door, to the other side of the block. And Jury, with every effort, followed. Because the two pursuers didn't give up as quickly as he would have liked. They too stormed purposefully through the narrow canyons of buildings and could only be kept at a distance by quickly dodging around the opaque corners and projections of the many buildings. The employees of a commercial kitchen were cursing. They lost their balance in their white uniforms and fired off vicious curses amidst steaming kettles and dirty dishes. But that didn't stop the guys. Like a hunt, they continued on until, despite Tony's astonishing local knowledge, they reached a dead end. Another backyard, which served as a storage and dumping area,

surrounded by high walls. Tony stopped, and when Jury had some breathing room, he tried again:
"You know, I don't know what they want either. But they 've been following me for a while," he groaned.
"Yeah, no problem. We'll take a shortcut."
"A Shortcut?!" Jury snapped, almost mockingly, and looked around questioningly. To which Tony just grinned cheekily and asked if he could put on his GG like he did. As if it could basically beam you up. Like a new feature, a handy upgrade he just didn't know about. And while Jury was already doubting Tony's little sanity, he babbled about an app that was very popular among Realgamers. Especially among the spies. An extremely helpful program for avoiding exactly such situations. Jury made an incredulous face, but Tony had to hurry to send it to him via the glasses, and then they had to move on. Because the bad guys hadn't been shaken off yet, as could be heard loudly from the end of the adjacent building:
“Stop!” they shouted.
“What are we supposed to do?” Jury whimpered in despair, while Tony remained incredibly calm.
“We go paths,” he said, “that they don’t go,” and began to climb.

Assassin -like

Tony climbed a rickety drainpipe that led to an equally brittle and ominously creaking gutter. Jury followed as best he could. He had no choice. And as he watched a screw peeling from the weathered masonry on its way down, he looked down at their pursuers trying to climb after it. But it was impossible for them. They had been too clumsy. So that they had to shake the pipe, hoping to make at least one of them fall like a ripe fruit.
Jury shrieked as more screws ripped from a rusty anchor and clattered loudly onto the hard stone floor of the backyard. Tony reached out a hand at the very last moment. While he couldn't pull him up, he was too weak for that, but it gave him the support he needed to eventually do it himself.
"You won't catch us," Tony shouted, kicking a brick loose, which clattered dangerously to the ground next to them. The guys looked up in horror and threatened to continue chasing them. Because eventually, they'd have to come back down anyway.
Tony sprinted across the rooftops and whenever an insurmountable obstacle, such as air conditioning ducts, sharp-edged metal sheets, or ravine-like chasms appeared between the facades, he hopped and jumped over them with such ease that it was astonishing.
Naturally, Jury tried to imitate him. But he didn't always succeed. Then he had to catch his breath, rebalance his run-up, and gather a little more courage to attempt another jump. And Tony didn't waste any time, but hopped and leaped away, laughing.
"Wait," Jury called, until he finally stopped. Like an assassin, Tony gazed majestically over the rooftops and into the deep canyons of buildings in the catching sunlight. Suddenly, a reflection caught Jury's eye, and he could hardly believe who was standing in their way. It was the crooks who had apparently found an easier way up the many fire escapes to make their threat come true. Tony then started sprinting again. They were driven across the

rooftops like rats, which is why they couldn't stay together for long. They had to split up. Jury stayed behind and hid between a network of pipes that led to numerous black, maw-like service shafts. Tony dared a cat-like leap onto the roof of a terraced house opposite, which his pursuers didn't dare to take and tried to avoid elsewhere. A real chase ensued, over countless slopes, windows and tiles. But Tony was far too nimble, and when one of the guys thought, he was going to catch him at any moment, he cowardly jumped away. The result was that they split up as well, and one of the two ran back towards Jury. Luckily, they had their glasses with them and were able to exchange information about their whereabouts.

On the other side, where the houses were slightly higher up, Tony had a better view, so Jury asked him for help when one of them approached him angrily. A rough-looking man with ripped jeans and tattoos on his knuckles, tightening the escape circle. Tony suggested climbing into a nearby window so he could shake him off, because he certainly wouldn't dare follow him there. But Jury didn't like that. What if he was wrong? A ruse like that wouldn`t surely stop this guy. Besides, it would mean a new dead end with no escape. By now, however, he was getting dangerously close, searching for Jury with a distorted gaze. Looking for the slightest unusual feature or movement that would betray him. Crouching tightly behind a concrete ledge, with a steep drop behind it, he was in a tight spot. Except for Tony's window, just a few feet away, there seemed to be no way out. Jury quietly expressed doubts that this would really work. He wouldn't know his way around in there at all.

“I can guide you,” he heard Tony say.

“Guide me?” he wondered, trying to figure out what he meant by that.

"No time for chatter," Tony replied. "Go on, SG," he cursed, sounding exactly like Pimkin. In his haste, Jury quickly put down his backpack. He had to leave it behind to squeeze in more easily. He'd have to repeat it later.

Jury climbed through the open skylight of an apartment. Inside, it was cramped and stuffy. It smelled of sweat and cooked food. Cracked wallpaper hung from the walls and was gently blown up and down by a ceiling fan. From somewhere, the typical sounds of channel-hopping droned on. Jury ducked into a corner. Old, used household items were everywhere. He tensely scanned the strange surroundings for anything suspicious approaching and listened to Tony's announcements.
"Yes, ...stay right there," he said. "No, wait... go further inside, or he'll see you. Hurry, he's coming to the window," Jury heard, which immediately prompted him to crawl as quietly as possible, close to the floor. But that wasn't enough for Tony. Jury was told to leave the room and go to the next one. There was supposed to be another window on the other side of the apartment, which would provide the perfect escape route.
“Are you nuts?!” hissed Jury. Because who knew which sweaty guy in an undershirt with a baseball bat in his hand would be waiting for him there. And what if he even had a cute pet, like a playful fighting dog? "Then what?" Jury asked. But Tony remained patient and simply said that he didn't have to worry about that. Nothing of the sort was the case. The next room was safe. Just a cranky old lady in front of the TV, he heard him say. And as Jury crawled fearfully on, he wondered more and more how he knew all these things and almost believed that Tony possessed supernatural, even God-like powers. Maybe he was some kind of damned oracle, with a sixth sense and all. There is supposed to be such a thing. A child prodigy. “A damned freak of nature,” he muttered to himself, trembling with excitement as he tiptoed along.

Jury felt like an intruder. A criminal, gaining access to other people's homes, invading their privacy to feast on their possessions. Was this the life he envisioned as a Realgamer? Certainly not. He didn't want to be a criminal. But that must be what it felt like to have other dark machinations on his mind instead of gaming. Only he had no such intentions; he was simply trying to save his own skin. Which is why the fact of how he ended up in this situation was so elusive and, at the same time, exuded an unexpected attraction deep down inside.

Tony was right. The next room was a living room. A wrinkled grandma sat there, sweating on a worn-out sofa, staring at the TV. She must have been deaf, because the volume was turned up way louder than usual. But, to use gaming language, that played into his own hands.
Normally, he would have expected a more relevant, age-appropriate program. A talk show, perhaps, or a show about the devious behavior of the evil mole.
From the Eurasian Talpa, for example, which joined forces with the nimble weasel, thus perforating an entire ecosystem of meadow and wildflowers, and to protect them, an entire fracking process was blocked.
But the woman, whose age he estimated to be at least eighty, watched hot eroticism with brutal splatter action that left Jury speechless and amazed.
Muscular men with oily, sweating bare torsos, who slaughtered entire herds of zombies, first with machine guns, then, if they were still moving and making disgusting vomiting noises, with an overly long machete, before slipping into a vivid love nest of white veils with spry grannies.
Suddenly, the woman leaned to the side, searching for support, and stood up. It took her a few attempts, irritated by the strange draft that literally made her shiver. Even though the summer temperatures were practically crushing, especially here in the room.
Damn, thought Jury. Had those guys perhaps just climbed through the open window like him?! No, said Tony, but one of them would still be lurking there, looking for him, which is why he had to quickly move on to the supposedly safe exit. But easier

said than done when someone was moving through the room like a human steamroller with no way out. Only another spy tip from the spy saved him from being caught. He talked about blind spots that he had to use to remain undetected. Which sounded more like a farce to Jury than well-intentioned advice. But basically, meant nothing other than first cleverly hiding under a cluttered decorative table with an overflowing ashtray and shortly thereafter, squeezing behind a half-open door. All of this with perfect timing, of course, until the woman finally moved on, sighing quietly to herself about how difficult and exhausting everything was these days. And quite fittingly, the same thoughts flashed through Jury's mind at the same moment: *When would this day of deprivation finally end?* But there was no time for cry, as he caught the phrase on a carved wooden picture in the hallway.
The saying of the sophisticated drinker was written on it, and underneath: "*If you have beer, there's no tear. Is your gin dry, there still no cry*" it was written there, when Tony interrupted with new instructions, saying that now was supposedly the best time to slip towards the bathroom. To an open window. But how the hell was he supposed to know where the toilet was, Jury said sourly, and quickly scurried to the end of the corridor into the nearest open room.
"Don't go in there," he heard Tony shout. But it was too late. Jury was standing in the middle of a bedroom where a colorful canary began to croak loudly.
Shit, he thought. Why did every old person always have to have a vigilant pet? So he promptly threw a blanket over its bell-shaped cage to make it quiet. At least he'd seen that happen in a movie once. Unfortunately, the ball of blanket was too heavy and thrown imprecisely, knocking the bird cage to the ground. And just when he thought the creature's noises were already noticeable enough, he was now proven wrong.
The little monster croaked for his life, as if someone was trying to get him by the throat. But he just quickly put the cage back

upright and maneuvered it back to its right position. Food mixed with smelly droppings stuck to his hand and spread across the carpet.
"What's wrong, my dear?" Grandma suddenly rushed into the room, and Jury could only sink behind the bed as if he were fainting. This shattered the initial, reassuring assumption that she was deaf.
“What’s the matter, my little darling?” she whispered lovingly, not noticing the intruder in her haste, while her bird was screaming its head off and fluttering its colorful feathers.
Jury crawled under the bed. Slowly and quietly he moved forward until she noticed the mess on the carpet. Spitting gently, she pulled out a tissue. She tried to wipe it up and wondered what stupid thing he'd done now, letting out a deep, indignant snort. As if her body were crying out just as loudly: *Oh, if only I could bend down.* The back of her veiny hand touched Jury's face and smeared some of the filth right under his nose. He fought to suppress a cough and gasped for air. Dust swirled up. And just as he thought he might be able to survive the situation down here, protected by a blanket, the bird suddenly croaked these words: “Burglar, ... burglar,” came the scream from the slender throat and made Jury freeze. "What nonsense are you talking?" came the woman's voice, trying to calm him down with gentle teasing and some grain. And when the tips of her slippers dug dangerously close to Jury's stomach, she and her darling decided to bring out more powerful equipment to clean up the mess. It would only take a tiny moment, and he shouldn't worry at all, she said in a strangely exaggerated way. The problem would be solved in an instant.
Jury was filled with fear. Because if she came back, he certainly wouldn't be able to stay hidden any longer.
"What now?" he hissed, demanding Tony's help. Tony only responded with a groan and complained about his stupid move. And as Jury tensely awaited his next clever piece of advice, all he could get away with was a curt "F*ck you". This was followed by

an equally curt explanation that, in his own words, he would almost be blind and only had enough information for a few seconds. From then on, he would have to manage without him. However, he would specify a new destination before setting off there himself.
Jury didn't understand anything anymore. He begged him not to leave him here alone. After all, he had forced him into this predicament. Tony responded with brief, indecent words, saying he would have to get out of this on his own and instructed him via VC to open the small program he had sent him earlier. Jury didn't even know what he was talking about until he heard that one name for the first time: "*Pathfinder*"

Next Level Shit

Jury gazed around the room, fascinated. After activating the *Pathfinder* program, Tony had preset *Shadow Mode 1* for him. Whatever that meant, small, emerging lines, gizmos, and boxes suddenly lit up everywhere. Some of them filled with strange details as he passed. The origin and interpretation of the picture hanging above the bed, for example. What caught his attention more, however, was an arrow on the floor pointing in a direction. And Jury didn't need to wait for Tony's explanation to realize it was a path. The way out! Right next to it, a timer was ticking down. Only a few seconds, so the arrow got smaller and smaller. Then he started to look red, and before he could ask himself how that was even possible or even how it worked, a warning signal sounded, indicating danger. At that very moment, the grandma burst into the room. But in her hands, she wasn't holding a powerful vacuum cleaner as advertised, instead something better, as she claimed, to clean up the mess. In all seriousness, she was waving a powerful baseball bat and attacking Jury with it. "YOU little bastard," she hissed, and despite her age, swung a murderous blow. "You'll regret sneaking into my bedroom like that," she shrieked, her bird beginning to caw in time:
"Rape, ...rape," he chuckled, as Jury quickly jumped onto the bed to avoid her clumsy swings. And while she complained, almost inappropriately, about the now completely soiled bedclothes, she chattered about her neighbor, who had suffered the same misfortune. But this time she would turn the tables, she ranted and asked if he had been sent by those people who extort something as ridiculous as rent. As if everyone in this town, her dam hood, would naturally have known about it. But Jury had no clue what she was talking about. It had to be one of those crazy stories from days long gone, from her much too long life. A kind of lost side quest, so to speak, that no one has ever heard of. Which he also tried to clarify. But should he really tell his version

of the story, the story of real and Stationgamers, and also the Forresters or his unknown pursuers? Even trying to tell it would have been difficult and simply would have made no sense. Which apparently made sense to her too and therefore made her swing again.
Between the attacks, which she accompanied with a kind of battle cry and her pet with similar noises, Jury emphasized the action, remarking that it was rather unfair to attack a defenseless, comparatively scrawny boy with a bat. At which she simply stared at him determinedly, feeling downright insulted that a youngster like him had the audacity to compare himself to her mature body. And as she was about to launch another attack, she suddenly stopped:
"All right," she said, more demandingly than understandingly. "Then we'll just settle this without."
But first, he should take off those stupid glasses so they could at least properly look each other in the eye without all that newfangled stuff. She dully threw the bat to the ground, demonstratively rolled up her sleeves, and assumed a twitching boxer's stance. But that somehow didn't fit Jury's idea of conflict resolution. Did he really have to fight a grandma for that? How would that end? Probably no one, and certainly not him, would emerge victorious from this fight.
So he ducked deftly and jumped off the bed, hitting the cage and sending it crashing to the floor. This allowed the bird to escape. Fluttering wildly, it circled the ceiling light, where Jury saw a screen displaying its species and origins. He managed to read something about the jungles of Venezuela before two extended claws pounced on him. In a panic, he fled. He shot back into the hallway, where a new arrow on the floor showed him the way. This escape corridor was only calculated for him for a few seconds, a warning voice sounded, leading into the bathroom Tony had mentioned before, which had a small window open for ventilation. Jury tumbled over the windowsill cluttered with cosmetic products and shampoo bottles, back to freedom. But

before he could get there, he had to accept being caught by her. For a moment, his foot was stuck between the faucet and the sink, which she took full advantage of.
"Haha," she laughed spitefully. "Gotcha, you bastard," so Jury had no choice but to give her a gentle but confident kick. And as he turned around for that, another warning appeared above her massive body that he didn't understand. *Advanced liver cirrhosis*, it read, and just as the woman disappeared from his sight shortly afterward, this warning also disappeared when he was back on the roof.

He looked around tensely. Tony and his pursuers were nowhere to be seen, so he followed the glowing arrows the program showed him along the impassable paths between the rows of houses. Not only symbols, however; a clear voice also instructed him how to proceed. He was to crouch down and proceed at a crawl. He reached a flashing spot, wait there for exactly five seconds, which he was also given a countdown to, and then she said, "Continue," leading him to a new checkpoint. Straight to Tony's meeting point, as it appeared shortly afterwards. But he was nowhere to be seen or heard. Strange, Jury wondered, and assumed that he had already climbed down from the roof as announced. But when he asked if that was really the case, there was no answer, so he obediently followed the new voice.

Jury was thrilled. As he continued to creep, the program not only explored all possible nearby hazards and offered alternative routes, but also showed the positions and paths of his pursuers as they moved across the rooftops, searching for them.
Now, *Shadow Mode* became a more understandable term, which was more like stealth mode. The idea was to evade the enemy, move in the shadows, and use the environment to your strategic advantage. Even colored areas were displayed to ensure you always stayed out of their field of vision using clever live calculations.

Simply brilliant, thought Jury, suddenly feeling incredibly powerful against these guys who hadn't left him alone until then. They were getting further and further away, so instead of fleeing, he came up with the idea of setting up an ambush. But on the other hand, he wouldn't have had any physical means of stopping them, so he abandoned the idea.
He preferred to listen to the voice that spoke of a new corridor that would open up before him in just a few moments. But before that, protected behind a sun-bleached sloping roof, he spotted Tony skipping across the house opposite in distance. Jury tried to warn him, but it was too late. He was running straight towards their pursuers. But to his amazement, they didn't stop him or catch him. Quite the opposite. Tony stopped and seemed to be joining forces with them. Jury watched the scene in shock. He couldn't believe his eyes. Had he missed something? What kind of dirty game was being played here?! Who were these characters? Countless questions raced through his head until he noticed something strange again.
Tony hopped away shortly after and disappeared into a wall. No joke, so that he had already concluded that he had been caught by the grandmother and her baseball bat and immediately lay unconscious on the bedroom floor. Everything up to that point had been his imagination and his desire to escape. But why wasn't he shaken awake now, at this very moment, or had a doctor shine a light into his eyes to see if he was still alive? And the longer the situation lasted, the more he worried about his mental state. He even tried to feel for a laceration on his head. But there was nothing. Everything remained as before. How should he react? Perhaps he had already fallen into a deep coma, and where and when would he wake up from this nightmare? All questions that made him panic so much that he let out a loud, terrified scream. And out of nowhere, completely unexpectedly, the guy who had followed him to the old woman's window stood right in front of him. He stood there frozen, staring fixedly over the rooftops toward the horizon.

It was a dream. Jury had actually imagined it all, and as he fought back tears in despair, a familiar voice sounded:
"I thought you wouldn't hurry," said a spy, appearing just as unexpectedly in front of him with his arms crossed. Completely confused, Jury looked at him and took a few defensive steps backward, which drove him dangerously close to the edge of the house. Because he didn't want anything to do with him and especially not with those guys. "What's wrong with you?" Tony asked, practically urging him on, regardless of the danger. Jury felt betrayed, cheated, and abandoned, which is why he raised his hand and slapped him. But strangely, it didn't hit him.
“How did you do that?” Jury asked, even more shocked than before.
"What are you talking about?" Tony said, while Jury tried to explain himself. "No, man. I'm not real, you idiot," he ranted. "Look closer. I'm a fu*king projection."
"A... pro... jec ... tion?" Jury stammered in disbelief, taking a deep breath as he reached out an arm to him and it was true.
"Yeah, a shitty hologram, if you will. In reality, I'm already down at the corner. That's just my helper coming to pick you up. So come on, SG, follow me."
"But...that guy?" Jury said. "What about him?" and pointed at the person who was still standing motionless a few feet away. Tony couldn't see him, since he was just a projection of himself, but he made the correct guess:
"This, you weirdo," he retorted, he had brought it on himself with his loud scream, and spoke of a PP, which turned out to be *a probable position*. "Yeah, exactly," he replied to the questioning look. His idiotic behavior had drawn attention again and restarted the calculations to show possible positions of the opponents. And if he had paid attention to the number next to it, he said with another dose of reproach, he would have known that there were only a few seconds left before the guy showed up. "So, what now? Can we? Because we have to hurry," he added urgently, so

that Jury didn't need any more convincing and, just as he did, ran off to follow him over the rooftops of the city.

The Pathfinder program was a sensation. A truly breakthrough development that made it possible to feel like a superhero. Thus, the class of a spy wasn't as bad as Tony put it and complained about more than often. And as Jury tried to follow his projection as best he could, over countless obstacles, between and among the rooftops, in an acrobatic manner, he was shown his path in glowing footprints, which a gentle but steady voice gave instructions to imitate:
Jump from 20 feet away, for example. *A run-up of at least 3 feet is required*. Plus tips and tricks on how to use your environment to shake off your opponents, and much more.
A broad grin spread across Jury's face as, with targeted jumps and the persistent game of hide-and-seek, he finally emerged victorious and ran away unnoticed from his pursuers.
However, a new announcement came over his GG. It mentioned a security shutdown and that the program would only be available for a short time. Jury wanted to know what Tony was up to. This only put further pressure on him to hurry up. Because without this kind of support, he would have to rely on his instincts, which would be fundamentally nonexistent for a Stationgamer, he said figuratively, since Tony didn't strictly express himself so aptly, but rather expressed it in other, less gallant terms. Until Jury discovered a fire escape, which, according to the ad, led him directly to him.

Suddenly he heard a noise. It was running and kicking across a nearby rooftop, and when he turned around, those guys weren't there. Another man was sprinting towards him. Someone like a security guard, Jury guessed from his clothing, whom the old woman had probably alerted by now. But that didn't distract from the fact that something strange was going on. Gesticulating wildly, he ran after him. He told him to get off those rooftops. He even called him a dam crazy *Roofer*. It was dangerous and all that. But Jury wouldn't let himself be intimidated any longer, and he hadn't been *a Roofer*. He was dealing with a Realgamer. Determined, he ran to the ladder. Sure enough, Pathfinder had shut down by now, and there were no arrows, displays, or glowing prints to be seen. The instructing voice also remained silent from then on. But Jury no longer needed this help. After just a few jumps and a bit of climbing, he reached his goal and was able to finally shake off his pursuers.

Once he reached the street below, the projection merged with the real Tony, waiting for him leaning against a sign. And with this effective connection, the stress that the situation had undoubtedly caused disappeared. While they then made their way as planned to the nearest train station, where Max was waiting for their arrival to start the journey back to headquarters with them, Jury wanted to know everything about Tony's Helper and this strange program. Where it came from and why he hadn't known about it until then. But Tony wasn't giving anything away and preferred to play with his virtual dog by throwing an equally virtual ball in front of him into the crowded street for it to chase after, which is why only a certain amount of persistence ultimately revealed more.

Pathfinder wasn't part of a spy's equipment and certainly had nothing to do with Infinity, he admitted. It didn't do any medical scans or anything like that, no, he said. It only registered the person and could thus retrieve data. Data about the

environment, where people lived, and anything else that they left behind was logged and analyzed. Of course, this meant it could be exploited for dangerous and criminal activities and was therefore forbidden. And for precisely that reason, he ordered him not to say a word about it. Julius, especially, was not allowed to find out about it. He was never even supposed to say his name out loud. You didn't talk about that, he repeated. It was a forbidden word.
“You mean PATH-FINDER?!” Jury shouted, an echo rattling through the rows of houses.
“Stop that, you weirdo,” Tony hissed and continued to talk to him, otherwise he also wouldn't keep quiet about the fact that he had actually entered an apartment, not to mention broken into it. From then on, in some people's eyes, he would be a criminal and would have them, so to speak, in their hands.
"You won't do that," Jury said, horrified, even shocked by his callousness. A side of him he hadn't yet seen.
"Do we have a deal or not?" he asked, unusually calm. Stunned, Jury gave in so as not to upset a member of the clan. An influential member. Because Tony enjoyed the admin's trust. That much was certain. Otherwise, he might be excluded from the raid just like Finn and taken along instead. Still, he couldn't and didn't want to believe that he wasn't even allowed to talk about it or even mention his name, whereupon Tony finally revealed a little more. That's why it was also known among insiders as *the Mirrows Edge Chaos app*.
"Why Chaos?" Jury wanted to know, and Tony could no longer contain himself. This app could do more than simply query data. There was talk of traffic light and traffic control. Full access to driver assistants that opened up gaps in the traffic for their users.
"You mean," said Jury in amazement, "I could use this to simply turn traffic lights green or red as I pleased?!" To which he just nodded wordlessly, pressed a finger to his lips, and hinted at "a lot more." This is madness, thought Jury, and began to rave. But Tony reined him in. Because when it came to such illegal chaos

apps, there was really nothing to joke about. If you got caught, something like a robbery would be the lesser evil. Because not only the use, but even the mere possession of such programs incited the law enforcement authorities, who then carried out merciless enforcement. Hence the automatic shutdown. As soon as it was activated, access to an encrypted data set was granted, which was quite impressive. All movement profiles from fitness watches, smartphones, AR glasses, or similar devices, even the tracking of surveillance cameras in public places, would be fed live from it. "A real-time data octopus, so to speak," commented Jury.
"Yeah, something like that," he said, softening his remarks. Tony couldn't even tell the time from an old analogue clock, but he knew a surprising amount about this kind of technology and kept talking.
Therefore, Pathfinder was hunted by another AI, which tried to detect unauthorized access every time. A so-called *seeker AI*, and if it restricted the access radius too much, Pathfinder not only shut itself down but also uninstalled itself without leaving a trace on the device. You had to know that before using it. Otherwise, you wouldn't get much out of it, logically.
But that meant, Jury realized with disappointment, that he'd never be able to use it again, and he was angry about why he'd given him such a program in the first place. Hadn't he deliberately turned him into a criminal? Perhaps he'd planned it all in advance. He wanted to set him up and draw the authorities' attention to him. An attempt to get rid of him and kick him out of the clan. The latter, though, he didn't say. Still, it was a fear he'd had before.
"Don't be such an idiot," Tony retorted belligerently, having finally gotten him out of his predicament. He explained that if Jury couldn't keep the app active for long due to the shutdown, then logically it couldn't keep him active either. That's why it had to be handed over at the beginning, of course. That was the only way to extend the usage time. Everyone knows that.

Jury calmed down again and told of his absurd encounter with the old woman. The strange things she watched on TV and her talking pet in the bedroom. How he skillfully dodged the swings of a baseball bat, and all the insults she hurled at him. Tony couldn't help laughing when Jury repeated the bird's words in a similarly croaky voice.
Sure, she'd probably trained the creature to scare neighbors or people nearby, but that also got him talking about the confusing situation, where he almost thought he'd been caught by her. And simply taking off his glasses to get a better view of things hadn't even occurred to him. You'd become so attached to the device that even in retrospect, among the memories, you couldn't quite tell whether you'd been wearing them or not.
Yes, you really did have to develop a good feeling for what was real and what wasn't real, as Julius always preached and Tony parroted. But even if they had experienced a lot together, Jury thought, they couldn't become best buddies. Admittedly, his rude way of speaking didn't bother him. It was more the constant comments against him and basically all Stationgamers. Luckily, he hadn't noticed him trying to hit him up there. An overreaction on his part, which might have cost him not only his reputation but also his position as sprinter. Because Julius would certainly have been upset about that. His spy was too important to him, he had grown too fond of him, he had been on too many adventures with him and secretly Jury hoped that one day he would achieve the same status as him, or even a better one.
"Shit," he hissed and paused. Tony wanted to know what was going on when Jury mentioned that in his haste he had forgotten his backpack on the roof. However, it was now impossible to get it back from there. But Jury wouldn't be convinced and turned around immediately. Tony called him stupid. That they had already lost an incredible amount of time and certainly didn't have any to turn back. He could get a new one. Which shouldn't be too difficult with Flow, who always had that kind of stuff on hand. But Jury wouldn't submit to that. First, he had lost his gun

and now his backpack, and in Tony's eyes he acted as if there was something precious inside it. No, that wasn't the case, he said. Just some food and drink. To which Tony replied that the rats would have pounced on it long ago.
Jury grimaced sadly. Because for him, it wasn't so much about what was inside. Rather, this was something special to him. A gift from his parents. One that accompanied him to school every day and someone like Tony, who had never actually gone there, wouldn't understand. Something that reminded him of his former life and the only thing left of it, he blurted out. His only possession. But Tony countered defiantly that maybe that was exactly why he had to say goodbye to this old thing and that it was totally ridiculous that he was making such a fuss about a crappy backpack. He should be happy with what he had left and pointed at his glasses. His old life was over and a new one had begun, he said wisely, as if the saying had just popped out of his mind. Instead, he had stolen it from one of the many advertising posters in the area. He needed to look forward and so on. At the same time, Jury didn't want to be left alone in these streets again, so he reconsidered and had to submit to Tony's wishes if he wanted to continue this new life. But something else was bothering him, and he asked meekly to calm the waves of excitement:
“If all this data for Pathfinder was already filtered on some server,” he said, “who or what was collecting it?”
"Well, I don't know either," Tony shrugged. But it was clear to both of them that it had to be someone powerful, with a keen interest in such information. Jury finally gave his word of honor to keep it quiet. But a Stationgamer 's word of honor wouldn't be worth anything, Tony said cheekily. Then he looked at him and grinned. "Now hurry up, you weirdo," he added teasingly, and continued running. Jury followed him until they reached the station.

Like a Final Boss

Max sat on a stone staircase, which had already been walked on in a curved arc by the constant flow of people. Resting his chin on one hand, he looked bored.
He had sat down at the entrance of the train station, as agreed, to ambush Tony as he approached with Jury. It was immediately noticeable that Max wasn't wearing any shoes. His trousers rolled up to his knees, he stared limply through the crowd, leafing through a torn brochure with a comic section. His feet were practically black from the hot asphalt. People looked skeptical and, when the incoming crowd allowed, made an evasive swerve. Jury had already prepared himself to be the first to give a detailed account of everything that had happened to him during that time. But because of the deal he had made with Tony never to say a word about Pathfinder, he had to keep his account of his trip across the city's rooftops brief. Not to mention downplaying the fact that he had only gotten into trouble with two strangers and that was why they were late. Because Max was visibly annoyed that he had to wait so long and handed him his weapon without comment. Jury was overjoyed to have ZZ back in his hands again and immediately swung it onto his back by the strap. In return, he wanted to know what had happened to him that he was no longer wearing shoes and was now standing before him with bare toes, black with dirt. But Max made no attempt to go into detail either. Instead, he just wanted to get away. He would explain everything when they were on the train back toward the outskirts of the city, and he pulled out his ticket to head for the entry gates. He knew Jury needed it to get back like he did, so he tasked Tony with finding him at their old meeting point, and his guess was spot on. He continued walking cautiously, putting one foot in front of the other, constantly watching his step. Like one of those games of hopscotch, he seemed to attract everyone's

attention. Until they disappeared into one of the many onrushing trains.

Instead of hiding them, Max provocatively placed his feet on one of the rows of seats there. What kept people at a distance, in contrast to their gaze, was the fact that they were embellished with boastful words, making the story that had unfolded almost epic.
As if we were at the foot of a high mountain, no, even better, he said; meeting at its stormy peak, where we stood facing each other in heroic poses. The wind roared through the jagged rock, making your blood run cold.
- Well, it was probably the crumbling concrete and the draft from the many broken windows in this building, sure. But Jury and Tony listened intently as he continued his pompous rant, presumably inspired by the comic he'd just read. -
A readiness for battle flashed in their eyes. Hair blew in the wind. At first, there was only silence. Then a glare met a second, initiating the scenario that had long been inevitable. That was until a noticeable noise enraged the irritated minds. The sound of a flashing blade. Then a flash of lightning that illuminated the clouds of heaven. A final rousing of the surrounding forces, ignited in a single, but true explosion at the final clash of the adversaries.
“Was it a knife?” Tony asked, wide-eyed.
"No, man," Max groaned sourly, feeling offended by the objection. It was actually the dropping of a forgotten tool. "Yeah, maybe a screwdriver," he continued, echoing Tony's suggestion. A war of words ensued, with the usual accusations over who had started the fight first. Followed by her first attack. She moved quickly and jerkily. Each attack could only be blocked with a feinted move or a precisely executed counter, and the next one wouldn't be long in coming unless, deep in your cerebellum, you had the right impulse to ward it off. These attacks were so monstrous that it almost resembled a *Soulslike*. Those kinds of

bosses you had to study first to not only be able to defend yourself, but also to remain steadfast until the end.
Max talked about *dodging, hitting, parrying, rolling,* and *crouching*. All the things you had to master to beat this kind of bad ass, while he held Tony in a headlock, for example. To illustrate what the next and only move was at that moment to get out of such a situation and start the next damage phase. After all, you had to show skill here too, and it would have certainly brought in a big score for the clan. And not to forget to diligently refuel with healing. Which he literally did at that moment, gulping a cold soda down his throat as if he had already defeated the final boss of the raid, which unfortunately never happened. Instead, it was just a substitute teacher who had cornered him, like Jury before, and was annoyed that it was only through his constant calls on the glasses that she finally figured him out and had to turn them off purely for self-protection. He didn't mention the much too empty battery that he had forgotten to charge, as explicitly instructed by the admin.
Anyway, at the end of their fight, where, according to his version, he emerged victorious, they agreed to go their separate ways. However, she had foolishly recognized him as the same guy who had stolen from her not so long ago in a shopping street. And the only thing she felt was appropriate compensation for the tenner he had taken from her pocket were his shoes. The glasses would have been far too valuable for that, and he would never have given them to her anyway.
"But what did she want with those?" Jury asked incredulously, staring once more, like Tony, at his dirty feet, which he displayed just as freely to the other passengers with wiggling toes. He would have asked her exactly the same thing, he said. But it was the only on his body that corresponded to the approximate value, and when asked what she intended to do with them, he repeated her answer in the same vein:
"I'll just put it on eBay," she snapped spitefully. And when he hinted that he wouldn't let her do it, he threatened to go to the

police and report the theft. After all, now she could provide a detailed description of himself. So Max had no choice. But they had no clue how difficult it was to get by without such a useful item as shoes. It wasn't that bad, he'd thought at first. But they certainly couldn't imagine what it would be like to walk barefoot through these streets:
Small, sharp stones, shards, microscopic shards of glass that dug under your nails. Plus, puddles of urine in all shapes and sizes, from ovals to drops, streaks, and splashes. And if you skillfully dodged them, new, disgusting traps would open up.
Max spoke as if he were reciting the menu of a new exotic restaurant that had been opened especially for stranded aliens from the planet Krypton:
Dark, discolored patches that revealed disgusting things. From chewing gum residue combined with pigeon droppings, which had cigarette butts on offer as a topping. There were also crushed cans, sharp-edged bottle caps, and even dead, tangled rats, with their heads or bellies burst open, depending on the choice. Not to mention the steaming dog poop amidst the household garbage and cockroaches, combined with the slimy green saliva that people expelled from their inflamed throats with rotten teeth. There were also cuts, painfully bloody wounds where you tried to hold everything together until the abraded flesh fell just apart. And if there was even a tiny bit of unworn skin left, they had no reason to worry, because it would eventually be burned away by the heat of the roadside tar.
That's why he'd asked Tony to stop by their meeting point. Because, as Jury could surely now understand, he wasn't available to pick him up.

People with a barefoot obsession had always been a mystery to him, Max whispered. It was an eco-phenomenon that ushered in yet another stupid trend. Maybe all well and good on the beach or in a delicate meadow of flowers, but in the god dam city?!

"NO FU**ING WAY," he blurted out loudly, making some people turn around and gape. Syphilis, typhus, hepatitis, weren't these all illnesses that spoiled the fun of being barefoot? "Or was he mistaken?" he asked the passengers again loudly, whose disparaging looks were really annoying him and, as far as that nasty Eggersfeld was concerned, everything would have repercussions. At least he had resolved to make up for this loss of values as quickly as possible, so he promptly pulled out a squashed paper cup and actually started begging people with it. But maybe it was the many annoying looks that made him prefer confrontation. As the saying goes: *if everyone's staring at you, you might as well put on a show.*
At that moment, the situation seemed strangely familiar to Jury. Because that was exactly how he remembered Max the first time. Dancing wildly around, trilling a self-composed song to himself. And this one, now on this tram, went something like this:

"Look at it, I have black feet.
Am I just poor or seriously ill?
Give me your wages, because who knows.
*Is it the plague or just fu*kin cancer?*
The world is bad, so give me money.
This is how only the one who TEAIES is healed."

Despite this embarrassment, Jury had to act cowardly. He laughed unashamedly and at the same time wondered how someone could belt out such creative lyrics. Normally he would have avoided the situation, just to make it clear that he had nothing to do with this crazy dude. He might have even hinted: *What such crazy people in this town.* Especially when you entered a crowded tram like this. And just at that very moment, a familiar feeling came over Jury. A thought that had been with him for a while, ever since he belonged to a gamer clan: Because they were the ones. They were the crazy people in this town. And let me tell you something. It was just fine with him. At least he no longer had a problem belonging to a group of people whom, not so long ago, he himself would have looked at skeptically if they behaved in any way strange, different, crazy, or inappropriately. Because who knew what had happened to them in life, or perhaps even at the beginning of this day. And while he contentedly celebrated this thought within himself, he noticed that Tony remained unusually quiet despite everything. He stared at one of the train's many displays, where some kind of ads flickered at regular intervals. But this time Jury was startled when he discovered multiple copies of his own image there. A photo with a comment written underneath in red. There was mention of a reward, which suddenly overshadowed everything that had come before. Tony looked questioningly at Jury until Max noticed too and squeezed back into their row of seats. He let loose with some kind of saying, while Jury just waited for his face to replace by something else. Only then could he catch his breath and nervously glanced to the sides, hoping no one would recognize him. Max, on the other hand, was in a less tense mood and pressed on. Why they were looking for him so urgently. Jury didn't want to answer, initially believing that the elderly woman whose apartment he had sneaked into had already placed an ad. But Tony, who was obviously feeling the same way, pointed to a text that referred to his parents after brief eye contact. Therefore, he assumed they were probably trying again to find him. Max wasn't satisfied with that and started tagging the Forrester symbol on one of the seats with a felt-tip pen.

Jury’s thoughts raced. Because at the same time, it provided an explanation for why two strangers had been following him earlier. It had certainly been unintentional on their part, and perhaps a good idea in their eyes, to offer a reward for finding him. But his parents certainly hadn't done him any favors. Because this inevitably brought shady characters into the picture,

who usually had other things on their minds than just providing a clue as to his whereabouts. These types, who would probably have been called crooks or scoundrels, always tried to get something more out of it. Added to this was the fear that his friends might now betray him, too. Max clearly denied this, interrupting Jury's shared conclusion at the same time.
"Wait," he said. "How much reward are we talking about here?" to elicit a joking response from him. But Jury looked at him indignantly when he went even further, instead of pretending to be a spoiled rich kid. Surely a portly butler and even the scatterbrained driver were eagerly awaiting his return. But Jury didn't bat an eyelid. Whereupon Max repeatedly made it clear that he would never do such a thing. Treason was out of the question for him and included Tony in his statement. After all, they had reasons for being on the streets too. Not good ones, perhaps, but they didn't have to rub them in every guy's face. It would be perfectly fine if he didn't want to talk about it right now, and he could therefore take his time. And if he had any deeper secret, it would certainly be safest with them. He could count on that. Besides, he added, no one cared anyway, as long as it didn't involve a girl.
A moment in which Jury felt better again. After all, he didn't know Max's backstory either, and even though he'd often wondered about it, he didn't want to pass judgment on it either, and thought it best to keep his reasoning to himself. With the peace of mind that he had friends at his side who shared the same thoughts and at least a similar fate.
Suddenly Jury noticed that Tony's eyes were again staring, frightened. And so, it only took a moment before someone tapped Max on the shoulder from behind.

Second damage phase

"He, you thought you'd get away with it, don`t you?" a woman's voice sounded shrill and suspicious. Max turned around, startled. "Young man, is that really what it is? With your dirty feet?" croaked an old woman indignantly, immediately hitting him with a walking stick. "Other people have to sit there too," she scolded, so much so that Max lost his composure and snapped back. "Lady," he said, in a friendly, metaphorical sense. "Who would you rather let faust you? Hulk or Wolverine?" The woman looked at him in horror and replied that she would take on his two companions, whatever their names were. Jury had to laugh out loud, which made her even angrier. Luckily, she didn't get Max's joke and was more outraged that someone was standing up to her than backing down because of her spry age. And while they argued about who best embodied Hulk or Wolverine, or rather best represented his abilities, Max talked about the clan and how his companions were really just two annoying scroungers he had picked up by chance for a dirty temporary job in the gaming world.

"Wait a minute," the woman paused, pointing a bony finger at Jury, his expression crumpling. "I know you," she ranted, her eyes piercing, and tried to draw the attention of others on the train. Until Max intervened decisively and roughly pushed her on. "Outrageous," she stammered and stumbled back into the crowd of people standing there, who reacted impassively. So disinterested and preoccupied, engrossed in the chores of the day, that Jury felt confident again and admired Max's quick wit, who lately liked to dress questions with sexual innuendo in the guise of another context, like games or even a comic. A quirk he had clearly picked up from Ox, and he wanted to know if they had also thought it was that crazy Eggersfeld at first. The mood then became more relaxed again and everyone calmly took a sip from his already warm soda.

RAINBLOODS

The train descended slowly and heavily into the underground. Suddenly, it fell into night. At least, that was the impression, as the artificial light bathed the interior of the cabin, and looking out the window, one could only glimpse the facets of black masonry in the unfathomable network of tunnels. Suddenly, a voice sounded:
"Hey there. Did I hear that right? The Forresters?"
"...Yeah, and who wants to know?" Max replied as a group of three guys and one girl approached in overly fashionable outfits. Even the guys had wildly dyed, high-backed hair, tattoo-like makeup, and stylishly worn clothes, adorned with countless belts and studs that reached down to clunky shoes.
"We?... We're the Rainbloods," said one of them, who looked as if he'd just stepped out of a post-apocalyptic movie, and he talked about the event. How they'd come to this disgusting city specifically for this, and any Infinity Clan that stood in their way, whether in the game or in the real world, would get a beating. (His actual words were significantly different.)
Max admitted that it might be disgusting here, a cockroach-infested rat hole, okay, but as far as the event was concerned, they shouldn't get their hopes up or dream of anything resembling a chance, and he intentionally mispronounced their name. "We're called RAIN-BLOODS! Not Train- or Painbloods, you retarded gaylord," came from the girl, who was loudly chewing gum, trying to condense her insults by mocking the boy's

homemade junk, which looked more like a toilet pipe than a powerfully pimped-out weapon. Besides, everyone knew that they hadn't even made it to the next raid, the eleventh level, so they needed no further proof that they were total losers.
Jokes flew until one of them, a real giant, grabbed Max by the collar and pulled him towards him. Jury and Tony held him back. The situation escalated to the point where other passengers reacted, and finally, someone who would have been better off staying, pushed his way out of the crowd. In fact, it was the security guard from the shopping mall, on his way home for a quiet evening, who gruffly inquired what was going on. Who or what was causing such a fuss that the Rainbloods, given his rather impressive stature, let them go and began to make nonsensical statements. Instead, they invented some fun excuses for their own amusement:
"Oh no, I left my ticket in the crack of my ass. Arrest me. Please," etc. Another guy talked about how they actually belonged together. They were all basically brothers. “Right,” he asked, putting an arm around Max’s shoulder as if they were best friends and just had something to talk about. It was about gaming, Infinity, and the next raid. Something he had no idea about anyway, and something a department store security guard, as you could recognize from his uniform, would actually have to say here. But the security guard wasn't put off by the chatter and made it clear that they should either behave themselves or get lost. But he also took aim at the Forresters. Because even with Max, there was still some matter to be resolved, and he had "fondly remembered" Jury in particular, and ordered him, just like at their last encounter, to stay seated and not move. Max rolled his eyes, indicating that they should get out of there as quickly as possible at the next opportunity.
The train doors burst open, and as if on the signal, everyone jumped from their seats straight onto the platform. The Rainbloods followed.

"Dam, this city is fu*ckin too small," Max shouted, running barefoot into one of the tunnel-like underpasses. He ran between the people streaming in and out, over escalators, seats, and benches, causing trash cans to tip over and bags to fly. And once again, a chase ensued, one of such legendary proportions that it absolutely belonged in the history books, or at least in a gaming narrative.

Not only because it took guts to make such a sprint with bare feet on hard concrete, but also because it demanded a level of skill that simply astonished those who witnessed it.

At first, Jury didn't know how to react other than to join his friends, wishing he had a useful tool like Pathfinder back. A few arrows on the screen that at least indicated a direction would have been helpful, so he had to use his imagination.

Yes, he simply imagined it. And every time someone stood around stupidly or blocked his path, he imagined a glowing arrow that said: *Move down, right, or perhaps better still, go past on the left.*

Added to this were strange coincidences that, in retrospect, still seem unbelievable because, despite everything, they seemed to fit. As the three pushed through the crowd, a sober voice blared over the loudspeaker: "*Please, no running here," he said,* "how important it is to demonstrate good manners, etc., so that the unsuspecting passersby wouldn't panic."

But the good advice came too late. Like a herd of startled cattle, people everywhere jumped up, their bodies and their belongings blocking even more of the paths that would have been necessary for a quick, perhaps inconspicuous escape. Added to that was a group of snobby teens who lined up at the end of the aisle around a loud jukebox, blaring aggressive beats, which further escalated the situation to the point where even Jury got caught up in it.

He carelessly shot through the crowd. One example was a big fat woman.

- I know, some might say: *Another fat woman? Does this guy have a problem with them?* But yeah, what can I say? It was just like that. -
So this person, who he ran straight towards, swung a handbag with the sole intention of knocking him out and was only able to fend off the attack with a clever slide, a combination of ducking and an outstretched elbow.
The tough realgamer training of the past few weeks had paid off after all, Jury thought. And when he realized that it enabled him to fend off this brutal attack completely painlessly, he suddenly took a shine to it. It was really fun jumping around among people, kicking bags and trash cans over or away. In short, causing total chaos, as well as delivering targeted shoves and slaps. He even thought he heard the sound of a score at one point. A score that steadily increased with each successful move.
Nonsense, of course, but still cool, right? After all, the Rainbloods were after them. Whoever they were. Some stupid freaks, you know. Shadow dudes from the deep. From the stinking sewers, for that matter, whose group adorned itself with high-ranking names from Infinity. Or as Max also doubted, when he hid behind one of the many pillars so the rest could catch up:
"What were they called again?" he huffed as Jury arrived, lulled into a sense of security. "I think they were the *Pain-in-the-Ass Bloods*, right?"
“Yeah, I think that’s what they were called,” he mocked.
In short, it felt like they were in the middle of a freaky retro game where funky music blared and every action was rewarded with a cool WTF power move, plus a matching *beat-the-bad-guys -up* sound.
Even Tony, with an open bag flying in front of him and a soda can rolling out of it, showed courage and grabbed it. The owner looked horrified when he thought about picking it up, so Max just burst out laughing:
"Look at this; Little Tony has grabbed a power-up, " before quickly sprinting off. But the Rainbloods were unfortunately

unfazed by the chaos and quickly caught up. They didn't let themselves be left behind, right up until Max collided with someone, knocking them both to the ground in pain. And it took a moment, as they looked at each other, to realize, astonished, that they knew each other. Because it was actually Finn he'd collided with.

"What are you doing here?" he immediately demanded, to which Max countered with the same question, laughing as he pulled himself together. Surprised by such coincidence, that even Jury and Tony looked incredulous. The situation in question was interrupted by the Rainbloods, who threatened another confrontation. At least, that was the assumption. Because when they saw Finn smiling next to Max, they suddenly said, astonished:

"What?! You guys know each other? ...Come on guys, let's go," and with those simple words, they slipped away without any trouble.

Finn pulled himself together and looked into speechless faces. Because what did he have to do with them? A question that Max just asked him right away, probing with a big question mark, only to receive a curt reply that he knew them more vaguely than intimately.

The usual talk of a long story followed, which suggested that he wasn't going into any detail. Something that left more than Max skeptical. Jury also looked surprised, only to realize at the same time that, just like him, no one knew Finn's background story as well. The backstory. In other words, everything they experienced and did before they met and remained hidden in a shadowy place that was kept back, consciously or unconsciously, depending on the character. So he too had a backstory that nobody knew, and that Julius liked to call; *"Stories in front,"* when he talked about the difficulty of finding a suitable teammate for the clan. It always bothered him never be able to judge someone properly because of that, and ultimately Ox entrusted with this task.

Finn changed the subject to Max and steered the conversation towards his bare feet, which he once again had to explain. In return, Max wanted to know why he wasn't waiting at HQ for their return and instead hung around the city. Finn avoided this question by being defensive and didn't understand why they weren't in the middle of the raid at this time as agreed. Max explained that it hadn't taken place. There were problems he said, and during their exchange Jury realized how disappointed he really was. In contrast to Finn, who had a clear smile on his lips when he received this news and ultimately found out more about the whys and hows. Until Tony said, "I 'm hungry," and this time the four of them set off.

It wasn't far to the outskirts of town when they got back on one of the many trams, and Max mentioned the strange coincidences that seemed to be sticking to his feet like dirt that day. It really was strange that the two of them met at exactly this spot. They could have just as easily walked past each other. Fate had been kind to them, he said, and that what belonged together had finally reunited. Which led to Finn admitting that he wasn't happy about being excluded from the raid. He said he was fed up with the Realgamer life and had therefore set out alone. He tried to convince them that it was all bullshit. The whole thing with the clan, realgaming, and all that, even though he was actually the one who persuaded them to do it in the first place. But his disappointment was too great for him to simply dismiss it. The fact that they hadn't stood up for him also weighed heavily. To which Max suggested, as compensation, that they discuss the matter with Julius again, and if Finn wasn't allowed to come along on the raid, they wouldn't do it either.
"Isn't that right?!" he demanded Jury's approval. But Jury hesitated. He had been too unsure whether their leader would let himself be put under pressure by them. After all, they were the new guys. Dam SGs, as the rest still labeled them. But his friendship with the two who had accompanied him for so long

was too important to him to do anything other than a benevolent nod. So it was a done deal. They would only go on their first raid together. Otherwise, they would find a new pastime or return to the Alien club and their old lives.

The Forresters were together again. In the evening, as usual, they huddled around the fire at headquarters and, over a hearty meal, made plans for the upcoming day. The Eggersfeld incident had, as expected, had consequences, and after everyone had reported how they had successfully extricated themselves from the difficult situation, they considered what to do next.
Returning to the sports field was not an good option, nor was waiting until the following weekend. Time was far too short to postpone everything again. So it had to happen tomorrow. Here on the grounds. Whether the assassins noticed or not. Max's suggestion to talk to Julius again had also borne fruit. Finn was back! Except, as expected, Julius didn't like this approach, as he didn't like being bossed around and felt his authority had been violated. Although none of them ever wanted to undermine it. That's why he presented his sudden change of heart to the clan differently. It had been his inspiration to take Finn with him in the end. Because every player was important, Julius said. No matter how strong or weak. Finn had to promise to give his best every second and was secretly glad, of course, that the action at the sports field hadn't worked out. So the excitement of the day slowly subsided and as the setting sun bathed the factory hall in its evening red light, everyone was in the mood for jokes again.

Still, Jury was worried that he didn't have the power to truly compete. Everyone reassured him, and Max, in particular, put an arm around his shoulder and pointed out that his weapon ZZ, had already taken out a truly nasty boss. Jury didn't understand at first, until he rolled his eyes and everyone laughed.
The evening flew by. Ox had to endure a few more insults about his real name. But he was apparently used to this and simply shrugged off everything that came his way. Except for Max, and when he was already taking a breath to say something, he simply ordered him to shut up. So it was only enough for a:
“Klaus Kattowixz? Seriously?” Then Max made a typical eyebrow move and the topic was settled.

Despite their successful escape from Mrs. Eggersfeld, she had used all her power to her advantage. That meant that Julius was the only one who was no longer allowed to take a day off class. She had made sure of this with a long phone call. That he, Pimkin, and Ox were the ones who headed home earlier than usual. Everyone else, like Chris and Tony, stayed overnight that evening, and even Flow made no attempt to disappear into his hut as usual. They all got some blankets and lounged around the fire together. Because tomorrow was the day.

But while most of them were already dozing here and there, Jury couldn't sleep. The excitement kept him awake. And so were feelings he was trying to sort out. Because as he wandered through the city alone that day, he felt incredibly lonely. He had been helpless, and no one had really cared about him, and this debilitating feeling of loneliness only stopped when he met his friends again. From then on, it even tipped over into something else, which, even without his glasses, felt like a power and strength. And Jury realized that its source was this new community.
So he asked Finn to tell him what he'd actually been up to during their time in the city. But Finn didn't talk about Assassin Girl. That

was something he wanted to keep to himself. He preferred to talk about the drawing he'd discovered in the throne room. Fascinated, Jury was eager to see it, and luckily, the door was unlocked once again. Only the GG had to take it down, as usual, and take a light from the fire with them to see anything.
Jury tried to decipher the symbols, but when Tony happened to be strolling by, he asked him for advice. He explained that it was the level map. Using symbols, lines, and previously defeated bosses, they tried to get an overview. Because of the dynamic programming, the content was always distributed differently. Jury pointed to an empty square where an arrow marked level 11. And where he expected to see the face of a terrifying boss, there was only an illegible abbreviation, to which Tony immediately replied:
“That means the Horned One.”
“The Horned One?”
"Yes. One of the sons of the Glass King," he replied matter-of-factly, wondering why there was apparently someone on this planet who didn't know the story of Infinity. Jury admitted that he only remembered a few sequences where the details of the story were recounted. But when he looked at the map more closely, he wanted to know more about the enemies, and especially everything about the Horned One. Tony immediately began to talk excitedly when Max interrupted:
"BORING!" he shouted, pushing himself abruptly into the middle. Max wasn't interested in origins or history. At least, not if it conformed to his ideas. All that mattered to him was how to defeat an opponent. Their weak point, and he talked about something like kryptonite. "Everything else is just decorative," he groaned, yawning so loudly you could see deep into his throat. He made it clear that it was time to go to sleep. Max was right. Tomorrow was far too important, and Jury in particular didn't want to start it tired. So he lay back on his bed and pulled the covers over his head, exhausted from this eventful day.

Some eyes were open only a crack. The great fire still burned, and a blissful calm descended. Suddenly, the Forresters were startled up. Someone was clattering around. It was Tony, who, unlike everyone else, was brightly pushing an old barrel in front of him. No one knew what it was all about, and when the scraping and pushing next to the warming center finally stopped, he climbed up there and started talking without giving any explanation. The others were annoyed and far too tired, so they threw everything at him that happened to be within reach. But Tony wouldn't let that stop him. With wide eyes and in the blazing light of fire, he told everyone the story of infinity once again.

The Glass King and his Sons and Daughters

Long ago, there lived a king and a queen. Together they ruled a beautiful and vast land, with mountains, valleys, and rivers. Rugged gorges, vast forests, and even the sea. Where bustling cities and villages bordered fertile fields. They lived on a green hill in a palace made of glass. From there, they prayed to the gods and ruled the land justly and kindly. The day of their wedding was a celebration for all, and the people celebrated for three days and nights. The couple was overjoyed, and everyone at court rejoiced with them. With the arrival of the first spring, the queen gave the people new offspring, hoping they might rule the land justly and justly. She gave birth to two sons: twins who resembled their parents in every detail, both in appearance and grace. Just one year later, she gave birth to another pair of twins. This time they were girls, who resembled their parents in every detail, both in beauty and kindness. Another spring, healthy twins were born. But this time they were a girl and a boy, who resembled their parents down to the last detail in their justice and kindness. The royal couple, their children, and their subjects lived happily and contentedly for many years. But one unexpected day, the queen fell ill. She became so weak and sickly that she could only spend the summer days in bed. One doctor after another examined her and, after countless remedies and therapies, found no cure. The king became increasingly angry. He called on everyone in the land to make their way to the castle immediately if they could help her. The people of the land did as they were told. But every visitor, every new hopeful who thought they knew what ailed the queen, was disabused of this notion and had to give up after a short time.
From then on, the queen's condition grew worse and worse. Every morning, the king prayed to the gods to please help his wife. After all, both had always been kind and just. They had done everything to honor and praise their creative work. But no

matter how often the king pleaded and begged, the many images of his gods remained silent. None of the people, and even they, could or would not help him.
As it happened, the queen died shortly thereafter. The king wept for three whole days and nights, searching for an answer to his misfortune. But he couldn't. Filled with rage and hatred, he then declared himself a god and made his sons and daughters demigods, so that they could rule over the idle inhabitants of the land.
From then on, the king and his offspring terrorized the people. Amused by their insignificance, they cast off all humanity and transformed themselves into increasingly strange creatures with each passing year. The eldest sons thus also shed their names and from then on called themselves *Ogumul* and *Azillon*. Delighted by the meaningless existence of humans, the era was plunged into blood and darkness. The twin daughters were henceforth known only by the fearsome name *Tessidore*, and their youngest siblings proclaimed their power under *the Twisted One* and *the Horned One*. They, in particular, tried everything and waged countless wars to expand their power. The Horned One held a clever inventor prisoner deep in his dungeons to forge new types of war equipment and weapons for him. These included invincible swords, suits of armor, but also projectiles and machines as powerful as an entire army.
Even the ancient warrior people, the *Kasals*, who lived deep in the swamps of the *Narmus forests*, were enslaved to protect the walls of their fortress for eternity. No human child enjoyed this time and was often left alone between war and destruction.

But one unexpected day, almost a decade of terror had passed, someone fought back. It was one of the king's first warriors. A butcher of noble blood and his personal bodyguard, who had to watch as the once benevolent king transformed into something that seemed increasingly alien to him. With each year, the king shed more of his humanity and transformed more and more into

a creature. Like his glass castle, he too turned to glass. Like a disease, it started with the limbs. Then it infected the torso and then the neck. Until it finally reached his mind and finally the heart.
The warrior was sent by his king to fight many senseless wars. But when he could no longer bear the suffering and slaughter, he decided to stand up. He ordered his army to turn against the king and his entourage. And they obeyed. Like him, they cried out loudly. Furious with rage, they overcame the high walls of their fortress. They smashed the bodyguards in two. Guards who had also been bred to become terrifying creatures, and after a bitter battle, one of the *Tessidor sisters was* thrown bloodily from the throne. The king's former bodyguard lost his life, and his body was taken to a secret and magical place. But despite the pain and tragedy, those who lived there realized that even a demigod can bleed. Even those who proclaimed themselves gods were ultimately vulnerable. Not immortal.
And suddenly, the people gathered. They stood up to fight evil together. Fear overcame the king and his offspring. They quickly barricaded themselves and their entourage in the magnificent temples and fortresses, from where they could continue to rule the land. For behind the walls, their power remained strong. Heavy locks and riddles were intended to prevent those who would attempt to take over their kingdom. But selfless warriors, a few brave ones, set out to storm the sanctuaries and thus put an end to the reign of terror.

The years passed and the war raged. Over time, the glass in the king's body threatened to freeze him completely. But before that happened, he was forced to summon a powerful being who would defend the remaining walls to the last. It called itself *Sacoon*. It came down from far among the stars, and once unleashed, no power on earth could stop it. Consumed by madness, the king laughed, and when his work was done, he disappeared back into his chambers and was never seen again.

But no matter what terrible things might happen from now on, the people were no longer afraid. For they understood that it only took a handful of brave people, even just one individual, willing to stand up to break the shackles of tyranny and thus free every human being for all time.
"And yes," chimed little Tony. "These selfless warriors, these brave ones, that's us."

The gate

The Forresters were lined up in a line, facing a long, polygonal fortress wall with a large, round gate at its center. Tactician Chris had chosen this spot for this day, and he chose the parking lot of the disused chemical factory with its adjacent warehouses.
This time, however, everything looked a little different in the virtual world. Traces of the battle were visible. A bygone battlefield stretched out before them. Impaled skulls, crushed helmets and armor. Broken spears with blood-soaked flags fluttered in the wind.
Everyone had gone over this moment in their minds several times. Weapons and equipment had been carefully chosen, and their faces reflected a mixture of anticipation and tension. They were only waiting for the Admin's arrival. The punishment seemed to be keeping him there longer than expected. Some were checking their watches so impatiently that even Max was getting restless and fiddling with his new shoes, which he had received from Flow in a dubious barter transaction and whose waistband reached almost to his knees. "Don't say anything," he had warned Jury when he first glanced down at them skeptically. Because the resemblance to those of the Rainbloods was undeniable. Finn had also prepared accordingly, packing plenty of provisions and sturdier clothing, while Ox and Pimkin were merely working on their perfect setup and skill tree. The only thing Jury did in return was select special armor for the raid. Fit for a sprinter. Purely virtual, of course. Heroic black armor plates on a silvery background. Added to that was a shoulder section in the shape of two outstretched wings. Those of an eagle, which bore the Forrester crest engraved in the delicate lines of his chest and, not entirely unbiased, had a Roman style similar to Julius's. He, on the other hand, took an unusually long time to arrive at the agreed meeting point. Heavily grumbled about the tedious

tasks and his ignorant father, but then, without further hesitation, switched to gamer mode.

Julius stepped to the gate and held something up. It was the key that Jury, Max, and Finn had retrieved from the belly of a grudge, thus becoming members of this clan. He demonstratively set about placing the golden item in the keyhole. He had already extended his arm when someone nudged him from behind. It was Jury, who immediately said expectantly:
"May I?" Julius shook his head and said that this part was solely for the admin, and considered it his own responsibility to personally open each level. Finn then spoke up, arguing that it was actually their merit to hold it in hands now, and an exception could be made for once. At least when it came to opening a gate. Julius reacted stubbornly until others unexpectedly admitted that there was no particular reason why someone new shouldn't take on this role. Julius hesitated, and it was quickly apparent that he had no desire for further discussion at this very moment. After all, there had been derogatory comments about this very issue the evening before. So he sought Chris and Ox 's gaze until he finally gave in. Before he could act, however, their mage spoke up and, with wide eyes, demanded something, which this time he also felt no particular urge to do. But something that was expected from a leader. Julius gave a euphoric speech that not only instilled the necessary courage, but also a certain aggressiveness. He then rudely pulled Jury towards him and explained what needed to be done.

It was actually quite simple. Using *inventory sharing,* he handed him the key and asked everyone to step back. Jury held the small pyramid in his hands once more and immediately set about activating the large symbol. He only had to touch it, and something inside began to work noisily.
Everyone stared, spellbound, at the gate and its symbols, which began to change in a subtle way. The many shapes and lines

gradually transformed into a powerful gear. This, in turn, seemed to be part of a hidden mechanism, rattling mysteriously behind it. Tactician Chris whispered that the level was now being calculated. The servers needed a moment to evaluate all the environmental data, where an AI performed the complex calculations.
The countless small levers, cogs, and force transmitters continued to turn incessantly until they steadily slowed down and reached a predetermined target. A shattering "*clack* " and "*clong*" sounded, and everything that had become embedded there over time broke and crumbled away. It trickled to the ground like sand. Then, after a silence, the moment had finally come. The gate opened.
At first, only a crack was visible. Behind it, a soft, sun-drenched glow. Then a blindingly bright beam of light shot out, slowly creeping toward them. Jury stepped back, for it was so bright that it consumed everything. Then it took a moment before the gate clicked into its final position with a loud groan and a shuddering thud. The way to Level 11 was clear.

"***Welcome warriors and fools***",

a deep, raspy voice sounded from the background. No one moved. Silently, everyone stared into the light, which blocked the view inside, and remained standing on the dreary ground of the parking lot, where garbage and sun-bleached paper still blew across. And just a few steps away, like a precisely drawn line that marked a boundary, was the entrance to a new, unknown world. Another moment passed before someone spoke up:
"Who goes first?"
With this sentence, everyone looked at Jury as if they were telling him that this was finally his level. Even Julius nodded, indicating that he should now have the courage to take the first step. But it wasn't until Jury received a firm nudge from Max that he started moving.

Jury gripped his weapon ZZ tightly and moved forward slowly. And only when he was within a few steps of the gate did the miraculous transformation begin. A transformation like no other. Jury looked down at himself, and with just one more step, first his shoes, then all the way up to his legs, were covered in an impressive texture. But it wasn't just visible, it was audible too. Like a mechanical combat suit made of an unknown, perhaps otherworldly material, he was encased in small, sophisticated armor plates. And when he stopped moving, this transformation also stopped. When he moved on, it continued, as it were. He looked in amazement not only at his hands, how their new appearance made them appear incredibly powerful. Besides his weapon, which had previously been a rusty frame, his entire being had changed. There was no sign of the scrawny boy standing in an equally filthy parking lot in his dirty, torn clothes. Truly, before this mystical transition, he had now matured into an impressive warrior who still had to prove himself.
So Jury paused one last time. Shadows stirred in the radiant light. Was it merely a fluctuation? A ripple from the source? Or perhaps the danger looming behind it? He looked back tensely, where the others waited, spellbound, their faces expectant. Then he aimed his weapon, ready to pull the trigger. For something could have sprung from it in an instant. A creature. A monster of unknown origin, catapulting itself straight into his world, landing on the asphalt, the still-visible street, and hurling itself at him with a wild roar. But everything remained silent, and I would have loved to say that flashes of lightning shot out from it. Trembling and igniting at the same time. But all that could be heard was a faint whisper of the radiant light. Nevertheless, courage had to be summoned from within. One more deep breath, and then it finally happened. Jury stepped into the light and saw fantastic things.

Sequel follows...

The story continues

next part
Gamers - first Raid -

STRUCTURE OF GAMERS

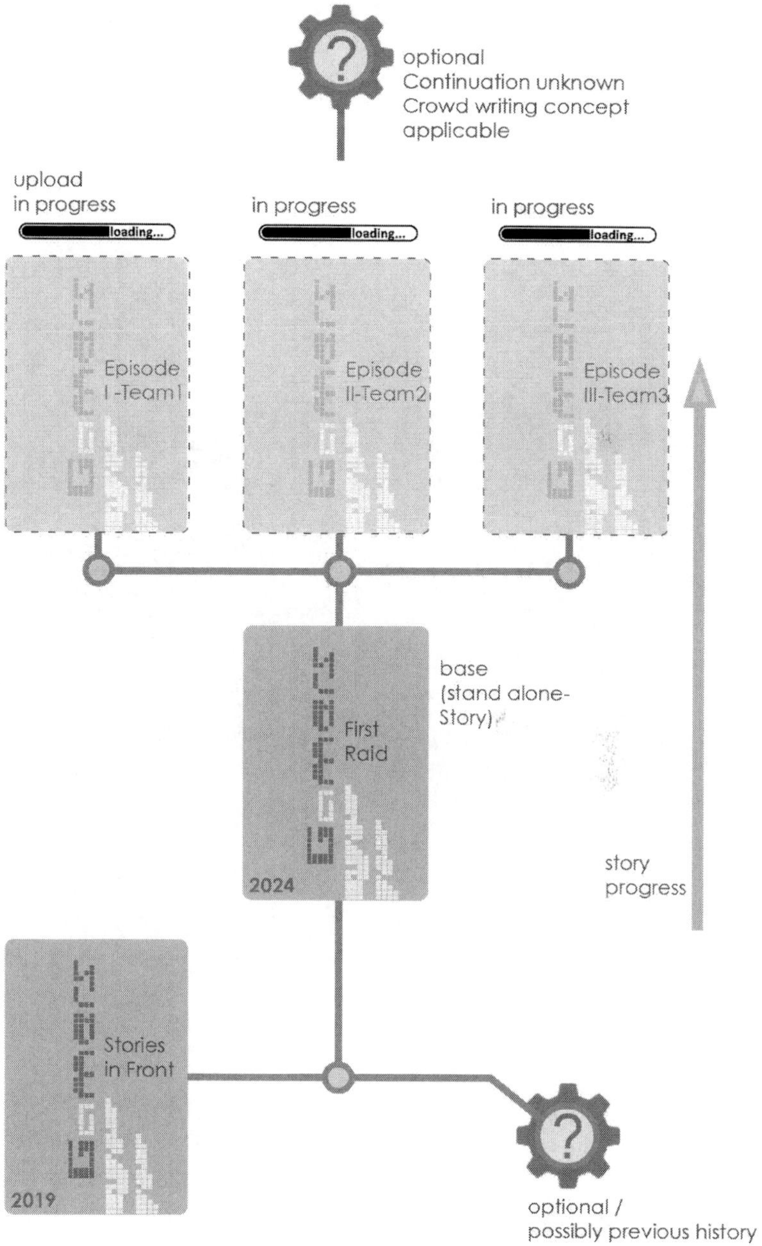

— AUGMENTED REALITY GLASSES —

HANDOUT

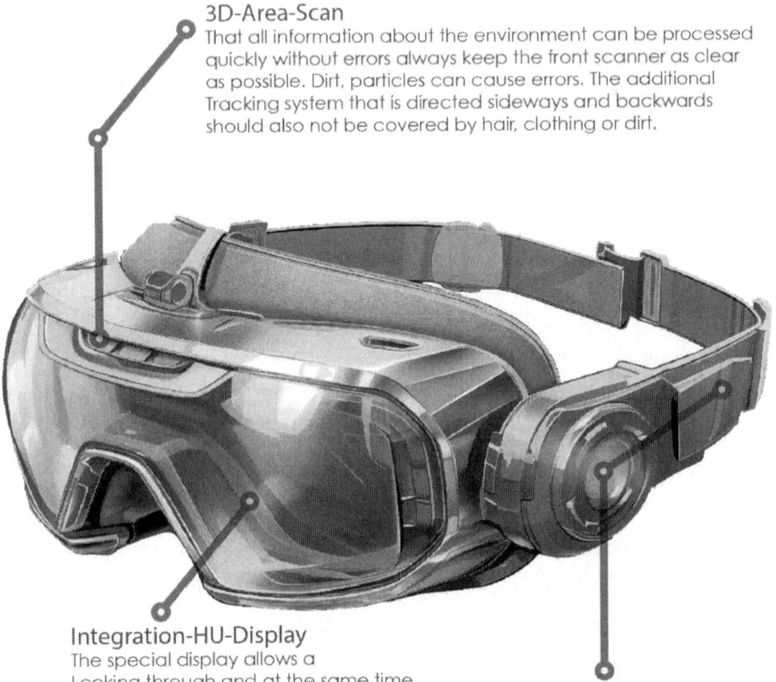

Printed in Poland
by Amazon Fulfillment
Poland Sp. z o.o., Wrocław

51825512R00120